THE VOODOO PLOT

THE
VOODOO PLOT

Franklin W. Dixon

Illustrated by Leslie Morrill

WANDERER BOOKS

Published by Simon & Schuster, New York

Published by WANDERER BOOKS
A Simon & Schuster Division of
Gulf & Western Corporation
Simon & Schuster Building
1230 Avenue of the Americas
New York, New York 10020

Manufactured in the United States of America
10 9 8 7 6 5 4 3 2 1

THE HARDY BOYS is a trademark of Stratemeyer Syndicate,
registered in the United States Patent and Trademark Office

WANDERER and colophon are trademarks of Simon & Schuster

Library of Congress Cataloging in Publication Data

Dixon, Franklin W.
The voodoo plot.

(The Hardy boys mystery stories; 72)
Summary: While in New Orleans during Mardi
Gras, the two young sleuths try to track down the
perpetrators of a rash of burglaries.
[1. Mystery and detective stories] I. Morrill,
Leslie H., ill. II. Title. III. Series: Dixon,
Franklin W. Hardy boys mystery stories; 72.
PZ7.D644Vo   [Fic]   81-21800
ISBN 0-671-42350-9   AACR2
ISBN 0-671-42351-7 (pbk.)

Contents

1 The Stakeout

Frank and Joe Hardy stood at the door to their father's study. Having just returned from shooting baskets at the neighborhood basketball court, both boys were still in their sweat suits when they heard their names called. Joe, blond-haired and a year younger than his brother Frank, carried a ball under his arm.

Inside the study, Fenton Hardy sat behind his desk, mulling over a pile of papers. Another man was seated in front of him.

"IIi, Dad," Frank said, drawing his father's attention. "What did you want us for?"

Mr. Hardy looked up and nodded toward the stranger. "Boys, this is Mr. Durby McPhee," he introduced the tall, red-haired man. "He owns an art gallery and antique shop in town."

"Oh, yes, we know the place," Frank put in. "McPhee's Antiques on Baker Street. Aunt Gertrude loves to go in there and browse around."

McPhee stood up and extended a pale, bony hand to Frank and Joe. "I hear you are following in your father's footsteps and have become good detectives," he said, shaking their hands. "That's why I'm here. I'd like to hire you for tonight."

"What would you like us to do?" Joe asked.

"Watch my gallery. I'm having an alarm system installed, but it won't be ready till tomorrow. Have you heard about the string of gallery thefts throughout the country?"

"Yes," Frank replied. "We know Dad's just started working on that case."

"Right," McPhee said. "Chief Collig told me this morning. There's been a lot of trouble in several states. What you might not know is that the Art Deco Gallery in Lewiston was burglarized last night. Over fifty thousand dollars worth of silver and paintings were stolen. Art Deco is the only other gallery in a ten-mile radius from here, and I'm worried that my place will be next on the list."

"I can understand that," Frank said.

"What's more," McPhee continued, "I've seen a

8

funny-looking guy hanging around my place for the last few days."

"Funny-looking?" Frank questioned.

"Yes. He was wearing a tricornered hat."

"A tricornered hat?" Joe blurted. "Those things went out of style a couple of hundred years ago!"

McPhee threw his hands up. "I know it sounds crazy, but that's what I saw."

"And you suspect this man was casing your gallery?" dark-haired, eighteen-year-old Frank inquired.

The man shrugged. "Could be, couldn't it?"

"I think anyone staking out a target for a burglary would be dressed less conspicuously," Joe suggested.

Again McPhee shrugged. "Maybe the guy's a nut. All I know is, I'm worried, and I'd feel better if I had a couple of guards. The alarm people promised me the system would be working tomorrow, but I have a feeling it will take a couple more days."

Joe grinned. "Actually, we have promised our dates a visit to the traveling carnival in Bayport Meadows tomorrow night."

"Won't they take a raincheck?"

"Oh, I think they will, if need be."

"Good. Anyway, it might only be for tonight. Will you take the job?"

9

"We'll be glad to," Frank said. "We have exams tomorrow but we can quiz each other in the car while we're on the stakeout, right, Joe?"

Joe nodded. "It's midterm exams," he explained. "After tomorrow morning and a basketball game in the afternoon, we'll be on spring vacation. Then we'll have more time to help Dad on the case."

Fenton Hardy, once the star basketball player of his high school, beamed with pride for his two sons. "My boys are too modest," he told McPhee. "The game they're playing tomorrow is for the area championship."

"I'm impressed!" McPhee said with a grin. "Maybe I'll come and watch them win."

"To get back to your problem," Frank changed the subject, "have you called the police?"

McPhee shook his head. "They won't be able to help if all I have is a suspicion. Sure, I could perhaps get them to send a patrol car by my place more often during the night, but that's not enough. I feel safer with you watching the gallery. Now, none of the other burglaries were committed after midnight. So you can go home, say, at twelve-thirty."

Frank turned to his father. "Isn't that odd, Dad— the time factor, I mean?"

"Not really," replied the famous investigator, who had gained his extensive experience on the

New York City Police Force. "You see, once traffic dies down and the streets become empty, the burglars are more likely to attract the attention of patrolling police. It seems these people prefer to operate just after it gets dark, but the streets are still busy. Since they've stolen antique furniture as well as paintings, silver, and jewlery, they had to load a truck. That could be done more inconspicuously when the streets were still alive with activity."

Mr. McPhee excused himself for a moment, while Mr. Hardy discussed the best spot for the stakeout with the boys. Soon after that, the detective showed the antique dealer to the door, promising that the boys would be on the job right after dinner.

Once they had showered and eaten, Frank and Joe grabbed their books and got into their yellow sports sedan. Darkness was just about to fall over Bayport by the time they arrived in the busy part of the city, where McPhee's gallery was located.

The boys parked diagonally across the place in front of a fast-food restaurant, where their car would not arouse the suspicion of any would-be thieves.

"What about the back of the place?" Joe asked his brother. "I'm sure any prospective burglars wouldn't load through the front entrance."

"That's right," Frank replied. "They'd pull their truck up to the rear parking lot. I'm going out there now to check if anyone's there. If not, we'll see them drive in. They have to go through that driveway on the left. There's no other access to the parking lot."

He got out of the car and strolled across the street. He surveyed the gallery thoroughly and convinced himself that no strangers were anywhere near it. Then he rejoined Joe and they started quizzing each other for the next day's exams, all the while keeping an eye on McPhee's Antiques.

After an hour, they took a break from their studies, and Joe went into the restaurant to get sodas. When he came out again, he resumed questioning Frank. He read from the book with a small flashlight, while his brother kept the driveway under surveillance as he answered.

"What were the revolutionary soldiers called who stood ready to leave their homes to fight when Paul Revere gave them the signal?" Joe quizzed.

"The Minutemen," Frank answered correctly.

"And when did James Oglethorpe bring refugees from English prisons to Georgia?"

"Seventeen thirty-three."

"Good," Joe said. "Now, what river did George Washington cross—"

"Turn off the flashlight!" Frank cried in a whisper as he grabbed his brother's arm. "I saw someone."

Joe did so and scanned the dark street. Suddenly,

a man darted into the driveway of the gallery with a sack over his shoulder.

"Let's get him!" Joe cried out.

"Right!"

Both boys hopped from the car and bolted for the parking lot. But when they arrived there, the man was nowhere in sight!

Frank and Joe stopped, dumbfounded. Then Joe pointed to the dense hedge that separated McPhee's parking lot from the property behind it.

"He must have realized we were after him and taken off!" he said.

Frank nodded. "Come on!"

They squeezed their way through the hedge and ran around the building on the other side. When they came to the street, there was no sign of the man with the sack!

"He got away!" Joe groaned.

"Maybe not," Frank said. "You go left, I'll go right. We'll meet at the car later."

Frank sped off, hoping to see the man at the next intersection. However, he had no luck. The guy must have escaped in between the buildings, unless Joe is more successful in catching him, the boy said to himself. Disappointed, he returned to their car. Joe appeared a few moments later. He had not caught the mysterious figure either.

Just then, the Hardys noticed a policeman whom

they knew well coming out of McPhee's gallery. They ran over to him apprehensively.

"Is anything wrong, Officer Gillis?" Frank asked.

"I'm not sure. When I walked by, I saw that the door was ajar. I called Mr. McPhee. He's on his way over."

Frank and Joe had a sinking feeling in the pits of their stomachs. Had someone broken into the gallery while they were chasing the man with the sack?

Just then, McPhee arrived. He brushed past the boys and the policeman and ran into his shop. Moments later, he rushed out again in great agitation.

"I've been robbed!" he cried. "An antique silver service and three very valuable canvases are gone!" He glared at the Hardys. "What happened?"

"We were sidetracked, Mr. McPhee," Frank admitted and quickly told about the man with the sack whom they had followed.

"And you're supposed to be such great detectives!" McPhee spat. "That's what I get for trusting a couple of kids!" He ran into his shop again, muttering and fuming, then came out, locked the door, and drove off.

"The lock wasn't broken?" Frank asked the officer.

"No. The burglar slipped in a window in the back. It was rather small and high up. He must have

14

been a circus acrobat to get through there, and very thin at that." Officer Gillis shook his head in wonder, then said, "Can you come down to headquarters around seven in the morning? We'll need a full report from you."

"Sure thing," Joe promised. Then the officer left and the boys returned to their car.

"Come to think of it, did you see what that creep who fooled us had on?" Joe grumbled.

"How could I miss it?" Frank said, referring to the large, tricornered hat the man had worn. "Must have been the same guy McPhee spotted earlier. I couldn't see his face, though. Could you?"

"Not at all." The blond boy sighed. "He had that hat pulled down too far. Anyway, it was too dark to get a good look at him."

Frank nodded and opened the car door. He was just about to slide behind the wheel when he stopped short. He jumped away as the car's interior was suddenly filled with a chorus of rattles!

2 "Don't Tread on Me!"

"Shut the door!" Joe shouted at his brother, who stood with his mouth gaping at the sight before him.

The car was filled with rattlesnakes! The strange noise originated in their tails, a sign of warning that they were ready to strike. Two of the serpents lay coiled on the front seat, several more were on the floor, and one was draped over the backrest on the passenger side.

Frank came to his senses and slammed the door, trapping the dangerous reptiles inside. "How did *they* get here?" he gasped.

"I bet the creep with the tricornered hat dropped them off after he burglarized the gallery!" Joe muttered. "He must have known Dad is working on

the case. Perhaps he staked out our house and followed us here."

"Well, we can't drive home with those critters in the car," Frank said. "Maybe Dad can pick us up."

He went to the phone booth in the restaurant and called his father, but the line was busy, so he decided to try their friend Chet Morton. Chet was a plump, good-natured boy who had often joined the Hardys in solving mysteries.

"Sounds like you have a crazy guy out to get you," Chet said when he heard the story. "I'll be there as soon as I can."

Frank and Joe were sitting on the curb next to the car when Chet's jalopy putt-putted down Baker Street. He immediately got out and went to look at the snakes.

"They're mean-lookin' critters all right," he said, mimicking a hillbilly accent. "You boys ought to be mo' careful around these here parts. Them hills are chock full of rattlers tryin' to hitch a ride out o' town."

Frank laughed. "And you're chock full o' hot air. But one thing's for sure. If anyone tries to steal our car tonight, he's in for a nasty surprise."

The trio climbed into Chet's jalopy and headed back to the Hardy house. When their father opened the door, they could see in his face that he already knew what had happened.

"McPhee called and told me," he said. "He was very upset. I'd like to hear your side."

"We were fooled into chasing a guy with a sack and a tricornered hat while the gallery was broken into," Frank said. "And to top it all off, we think he left us a little memento in our car. A bunch of rattlesnakes!"

"What?" Mr. Hardy looked dumbfounded.

After the boys had told him the whole story, the detective shook his head. "Well, it certainly seems like that man in the tricornered hat is connected with the burglaries. I'll have to check into the other cases and see if someone like that was spotted. As you know, I just started working on this and I haven't had a chance to go through all the files yet."

"What I want to know," Joe wondered aloud, "is where those snakes came from. It seems like a pretty bizarre way of getting rid of us. Besides, you can't just pick up a bunch of rattlesnakes at your local pet store. I've never even seen any in this area, except at the zoo."

"And that's the first place we're going tomorrow after our exams," Frank said. "Not only do we need an explanation about the snakes' origin, but we also have to find someone who can get them out of our car."

Frank, Joe, and Chet discussed the mystery for a while longer, then their friend drove home and the young detectives went to bed. They were awakened early the next day to the sound of a woman's voice coming from the first floor.

Aunt Gertrude, the Hardy's live-in aunt, was speaking in a loud, scolding tone. She was often stern with Frank and Joe, even though deep down she had great admiration for their sleuthing skills. But this morning her words were directed at someone else. The brothers bounded down the stairs, curious to see what the problem was.

"But it has to be somewhere!" Aunt Gertrude was grumbling as the boys entered the kitchen. The tall, angular woman stood with her hands on her hips, looking down at Mr. Hardy, who sat at the table hiding behind a newspaper. "And you'd better find it!"

"Good morning!" Fenton Hardy greeted his sons enthusiastically, relieved to have them in the kitchen. "It seems we have another mystery on our hands. I have been accused of misplacing one of my socks." With this, the sleuths' father gave Frank and Joe a wink and a sly grin while holding his newspaper up to his face, angled so that his sister couldn't see him.

"Hah!" Miss Hardy exclaimed. "Your father, the great detective, has lost one of a perfectly good pair of socks. And he tells me he looked everywhere and can't find it. I suppose it just got up and walked away of its own accord!"

Frank and Joe had to fight back smiles as they pretended to take the matter seriously. "We'll look for it, Aunt Gertrude," Frank promised, and while she fixed scrambled eggs, the boys searched the house. They checked underneath Mr. Hardy's dresser, in the laundry baskets, and behind the automatic washer. But by the time their aunt called them back to the kitchen, they still hadn't found the missing sock.

After breakfast, the brothers collected their books and stopped off at police headquarters, where they made a detailed report of the previous night's events. Then they continued on to school. Their exams were over by late morning, and both felt they had done well. They were bothered, however, by the fact that Peter Walker, a classmate of Joe's and the star of the basketball team, had not shown up for school that morning.

"I hope he's not sick," Joe said as they left the building.

"Me, too," Frank agreed. "We haven't a chance of winning the championship without Peter."

"Hey, guys!" Chet called out as he ran down the front steps to catch up with his buddies. "How did you do on your exams?"

Both Hardys were "A" students at Bayport High, but Chet averaged mostly Bs and Cs. He was bright, but a little lazy about his studies.

"Fine," Frank answered, stopping to let his chubby friend join them. "How about you?"

Chet winced. "I don't know. I think I did okay in the multiple choice questions, but the essays were hard!"

"Well, it's all over now, so don't worry about it," Joe consoled him. "Why don't you come with us? We're on our way to the zoo."

Chet brightened. "You're looking for someone to capture those snakes?" he asked.

"Yes," Frank replied. "And we want to figure out where they came from."

"Then let's go," Chet said. "I'll drive."

The three youths piled into Chet's jalopy, and in minutes they were parked outside the Bayport Zoo. The zoo was small but had a good reptile exhibit. The reptile expert, or herpetologist, was a young man recently graduated from college. He had light olive-colored skin, big eyes, and hair darker than Frank's. In his office, he listened to the sleuths' story.

"Someone purposely put these snakes in your car last night?" he asked with growing interest in the tale.

"That's right," Joe replied. "A guy who wore

a tricornered hat. Do you know someone around here who collects rattlesnakes and wears a hat like that?"

The herpetologist shook his head. "There are a few snake collectors in the Bayport area, but none who would have that many rattlers. We have quite a few at the zoo, though."

"Are any of them missing?" Chet asked.

"No. I checked this morning, and if any were gone, I would have noticed."

The herpetologist went into a back room and brought out a couple of sacks and a long rod with a wire loop at the end of it. With this gear, they drove back to Baker Street where Frank and Joe had left their yellow sports sedan the night before.

Using the rod, the herpetologist slipped the loop around the bodies of the animals and dropped them into the sacks. They seemed to be a lot less vicious than they had been the previous evening.

"They had a chilly night in your car," the reptile expert explained. "Like other cold-blooded creatures, when the weather turns cold, they slow down."

"What kind of rattlers are they?" Joe asked him.

"Pygmies," the expert told them, dropping the last one in the sack. "They're small compared to other species. Also, they're not nearly as poisonous. One of them couldn't deliver a lethal dose of venom by itself. But if several got their fangs into you, it might be a different story."

Frank shivered at the thought of their close call with the snakes. "Do they live in these parts?" he queried.

The expert shook his head. "Not in the wild. Pygmy rattlesnakes only come from the southeastern part of the country: Florida, the Carolinas, Alabama, Georgia, and so on."

"And you don't know where this species could be bought, or stolen, around Bayport?" Frank questioned.

Again the man shook his head. "I seriously doubt you could find any here at all. Someone had to import them."

Once the snakes were safely sacked, the young detectives searched the surrounding area, hoping to discover more clues.

"This must be the bag they came in," Joe announced after a while, coming into the driveway where the others stood waiting for him. He carried a large burlap sack. "I found it down the street, stuck on a tree limb."

"Look, there's a picture on it!" his brother exclaimed.

Joe spread the burlap sack on the hood of their car. Printed on it was a crude illustration of a coiled rattlesnake, and beneath it was the inscription: DON'T TREAD ON ME!

"What's that supposed to mean?" Chet blurted out, gazing at the strange picture.

Joe rolled his eyes at his friend's question. "If you had studied enough for your history exam, you'd know what it means. It's an emblem used by the American colonies during the Revolutionary War."

"Some bands of revolutionary soldiers had the rattlesnake on their banner," Frank explained. "Rattlers don't exist in Europe, so early European explorers to America were intrigued by these snakes, which rattled a warning before they struck. It later caught on as an emblem for the thirteen colonies, as if to say, 'We prefer to be left alone, and if you don't heed our warning to stay away, we will strike swiftly and mercilessly.' "

"Boy!" Chet said. "Do you think whoever put them in your car is trying to give you the same message?"

"That's what it looks like," Frank answered. "This guy in the tricornered hat seems to somehow identify with the rebels in the American Revolution."

"Maybe he thinks the Revolution is still on," Chet joked. "And he's stealing from the Tories."

"Hey! There's something in the bag!" Joe spoke

up, feeling a small object in the corner of the burlap sack. He reached inside and withdrew a glass vial. It was empty, but still gave off a strange scent from whatever it had contained.

"May I smell that?" the reptile expert asked.

Joe handed him the bottle, and the man took a whiff of its fragrance. "It's snake oil," he said at last, handing the vial back to Joe.

"Snake oil?" all three boys asked at once.

"Sure. Quacks used to sell it in traveling medicine shows. It was supposed to cure all kinds of ills, from rashes to headaches. Of course, it didn't really have any medicinal value."

"But that went out of style years ago," Frank remarked. "What would somebody want with the stuff now?"

"It's still used by a few old circus performers," the herpetologist replied. "They believe it makes them more agile, more snakelike, so they're able to perform better. You might be able to buy it from some traveling circuses, where it's sold as a curiosity item."

"There aren't any circuses in the area," Frank observed.

"No, but there's the carnival!" Joe said. "We're going there tonight anyway. Why don't we see if they have any snake charmers? Maybe we'll pick up another clue."

"Good idea," Frank said. "But now we have to get back for the basketball game."

In their excitement, Joe and Chet had almost forgotten about the game that afternoon. They all had to be there in time to change into their uniforms. Both Frank and Joe were on the team, and Chet was to play bass drum in the school band between periods.

Chet drove the herpetologist back to the zoo while Frank and Joe went directly to the school gym. When they got there, the bleachers were starting to fill with fans. Bayport's opposing team, Hopkinsville High, was already on the court warming up. A buzz of excitement filled the air for the upcoming championship game.

"Where's Peter?" Joe asked anxiously, looking around for their star center who had missed school earlier that day.

Frank scanned the court for their tall black friend, but Peter Walker wasn't among the players. "Oh, no!" He groaned, knowing that Peter was by far the best member of their team and the main reason Bayport High had made it to the championship.

With warm-ups completed, the boys sat on the bench with the others. All were as nervous about Peter's absence as the Hardys were. Among the crowd on the bleachers were the Hardy family and the boys' girlfriends, Callie Shaw and Iola Morton.

The girls blew kisses at Frank and Joe, who returned them with waves.

Then a roar welled up from the spectators as the players broke from the benches and took their positions on the court. Frank had to substitute at center for Peter Walker, who still hadn't arrived. The referee threw the basketball in the air and the game was underway!

3 Carnival

Frank jumped as high as he could for the ball, but the center for the other team outreached him by almost a foot. He passed the ball far down the court, and within seconds Hopkinsville had scored two points.

By the end of the first period, the scoring had left the Bayport High fans anxious and quiet. The bleachers on the other side of the gym, however, were full of cheers and hand-clapping. Bayport was losing to Hopkinsville, twenty-four to sixteen!

Frank, Joe, and the other Bayport players returned to their bench with gloomy faces. Without Peter, they were just no match for Hopkinsville.

During the break between periods, the Bayport

29

High marching band filed into the gym. Chet led the way, dressed up in a bright red band uniform and carrying a big bass drum with the school's name inscribed on it in gold letters. Frank's and Joe's spirits were lifted by the sight of their friend proudly carrying his drum and pounding out a tempo to the school song while marching in place. At least, they thought, someone was enjoying the event.

As the band continued to play, the coach gave his team a pep talk. He told them that they didn't need Peter to win, but that they would have to hustle. By concentrating on defense, they could keep the scoring down and also exhaust the opposing team. Hopkinsville might then begin to make mistakes that Bayport High could capitalize on.

With renewed enthusiasm, the boys went into the second period. Their coach's strategy seemed to work for a while. Hopkinsville was unable to make any points in the first minutes, and its members were starting to tire of working their way through Bayport's heavy defense. But Hopkinsville's coach suddenly realized what was happening and made up a counter-strategy for his group.

While Frank and Joe's team managed to keep the scoring down during the second period, they were unable to narrow the point gap between the two teams.

At the end of the period, Hopkinsville was leading by ten points, and the Bayporters went to the
bench in glum spirits once again.

Just then, Peter Walker ran out of the locker room
and headed for his teammates! The Bayporters
jumped to their feet to greet their star player.

"Sorry I'm late," he apologized earnestly. "How
are we doing?"

"We're ten points back," Joe told him. "Where
have you been?"

"I'll tell you about it later," Peter answered.
"Right now we've got a game to win!"

With Peter on the team, Bayport took control of
the third period. The point gap began to close
rapidly as the star center forward dodged and
dribbled his way through Hopkinsville's defense.
The Bayport fans were on their feet for the youth's
performance and broke into cheers every time he
made a basket.

Bayport High finally won the game by a margin of
six points. As the band played a victory march, the
team carried Peter Walker off the court like a hero,
not setting him down until they were in the locker
room.

"I'm sure glad you came when you did," Frank
told him.

"I'm sorry," the boy apologized again. "But I ran
into some trouble this morning."

Frank and Joe looked with curiosity at their friend. "Trouble?" Joe queried.

"My grandfather was supposed to fly in from New Orleans," Peter explained. "I went to pick him up at the airport before the exams, but he didn't arrive. I called him, and when I didn't get any answer, I figured he had missed his flight and would be on the next one. So I waited."

"And he never came?" Frank asked.

Peter shook his head. "No. I began to worry about him after a while. He didn't answer when I called, so I knew he was neither home nor at his club."

"He has a club?" Frank inquired.

Peter's worried look left his face for a moment. "Yes. Grandpa is a well-known jazz trombonist in New Orleans, one of the best there is." The boy's voice welled with pride as he told the Hardys about his grandfather. "He's known as Stretch—Stretch Walker—and he owns a club down there."

"Sounds as if you're a big fan of his," Joe remarked.

"Oh, yes. He's the greatest." Peter smiled before his face clouded with worry once again. "I really wanted him to see me play today. He would've loved watching the game. I've been bragging about what a good basketball player I am, and this was his chance to see me in action."

"Why don't you come to our place for dinner?"

Frank offered, trying to console the upset youth. "We're having sort of a victory celebration with the family, Chet, and the girls, and there'll be plenty of food to go around."

"Thanks, but I can't," Peter replied with a thin smile. "I want to go home in case Grandpa calls." With that, the basketball star finished dressing and left the locker room.

"He seems pretty upset over his grandfather," Frank said, closing his locker. "I wonder if there's something he's not telling us."

"I had the exact same feeling," Joe agreed. "He wouldn't have missed his exam and most of the game unless he was very disturbed. I can understand his worry, though."

The two drove home for the victory dinner. When they stopped their car in front of the house, Callie Shaw and Iola Morton ran out to greet them with hugs and kisses. Callie, Frank's favorite date, had blond hair and sparkling brown eyes. Iola, who was Chet's sister, had a special fondness for Joe, and her quick wit, liveliness, and good nature made her a welcome guest at the Hardy home.

The girls led the brothers inside, where Mrs. Hardy had prepared a delicious dinner for them all.

"Well, how does it feel to be the district basketball champs?" she asked with a grin as the group sat down to eat.

"Not bad," Frank replied. "I knew we had it in the bag from the beginning."

Aunt Gertrude raised her eyebrows. "Had it in the bag?" she challenged. "If Peter Walker hadn't shown up, the other team would have had *you* in the bag."

"Oh, Gertie." Mrs. Hardy laughed, her sparkling eyes lighting up as she addressed her sister-in-law. "The Bayporters won, and I'm very proud of my two boys for being part of it."

Frank and Joe grinned at the exchange between the two women. "Aunt Gertrude is right, of course," Joe insisted, glancing at his father who seemed somewhat preoccupied.

"What's up, Dad?" Joe inquired.

"I don't want to talk business, but I found out two things today when I worked some more on the burglaries," Mr. Hardy replied. "One, there was a similar string of thefts around the same time last year. And two, no one in a tricornered hat has ever been spotted before."

"Well, with Frank and Joe on the case, I'm sure the crook, or crooks, will be caught soon," Callie said.

Once dinner was over, Frank, Joe, and the girls got ready to go to the carnival. Chet volunteered to come along.

After thanking Mrs. Hardy for the delicious meal, the group piled into the yellow sports sedan and followed a main road to the outskirts of town. The carnival was set up in the Meadows and was glittering with lights and swarming with people.

Music and the smell of cotton candy filled the air as the youths entered the carnival grounds.

"I'm hungry," Chet announced, taking a deep whiff of the sweet odor.

"You just had a gigantic meal!" Iola told her brother in disbelief.

"I know, but I'm hungry again," Chet protested.

Frank chuckled at his friend's insatiable appetite. "Why don't you all play some of the games here?" he proposed. "Joe and I have to do some investigating for a while. We'll meet you later."

While Chet, Callie, and Iola went off to try and win some prizes, Frank and Joe scouted the grounds for signs of a snake show.

By questioning a booth attendant, the boys learned that there was, indeed, a snake charmer by the name of Gloria, who had a booth next to the funhouse.

Gloria turned out to be a middle-aged woman who worked with small boa constrictors. "Snake oil?" she replied to the boys' question. "I don't know anyone who uses that stuff any more."

"Have you ever seen this emblem before?" Joe queried, holding up the burlap sack with the coiled rattlesnake printed on it.

Gloria looked at it with interest. "Sure. It was something they used in the American Revolution, wasn't it?"

"Yes. But have you seen it lately?" Joe urged.

"Come to think of it, I have," she said after a moment's thought. "There's an old man in Georgia who tried to talk me into taking on rattlesnakes. He's a real rattlesnake nut and wanted me to improve their image as vicious, disgusting animals." Gloria rolled her eyes. "He was quite nutty."

"Georgia!" Frank whispered to Joe. "That's where the herpetologist said those pygmy rattlers might be from."

"Did this guy have any rattlers?" he asked Gloria.

"Plenty of them. Catches them in the swamp and keeps them in cages in his house, or so he told me."

"But what does he have to do with the emblem?" Joe questioned.

"He carried the snakes he wanted me to use in a bag just like this one," the woman replied. "Of course, I told him to get lost. Rattlesnakes I don't need!"

"Do you remember where he lived?" Frank asked.

"I think the town was called Swamp Creek,"

Gloria replied. "It was right on the edge of the Okefenokee Swamp. People told me he's quite well known in the area because of his strange hobby."

"I wonder what he does for a living?" Frank said.

"I heard he sells stuff at flea markets. You know, dishes and old clothes and sometimes furniture. Whatever he can buy cheap, I guess."

"Do you have his address?" Frank asked.

"Oh, no. But I'm sure people can tell you where he lives. Just ask for the snake lover who wears a tricornered hat."

"A tricornered hat?" Frank asked, staring at the woman.

"Uh-huh. I told you he was nutty."

After thanking Gloria for her help, the boys went to look for their friends and spent the rest of the evening having a good time at the carnival.

When Frank and Joe finally pulled into the Hardy driveway, their mother greeted them at the front door.

"You've had an urgent telephone call," she said, concern showing on her face. "Please phone Mrs. Walker right away!"

4 Snake Oil Clue

The boys ran to the telephone. Frank dialed the Walkers' number and waited.

"Hello?" Peter's mother answered, her voice sounding nervous over the receiver.

"This is Frank Hardy. We had a message to call you."

"Oh, yes. I'm sorry to bother you so late, but it's about Peter. I don't know where he is! He left home suddenly after dinner, and I'm afraid he's in some kind of trouble."

"What makes you think he's in trouble?" Frank said hesitantly, not sure why Mrs. Walker had decided to call them.

"He was very upset over something when he

left," Mrs. Walker explained. "He didn't tell me where he was going or when he would be back. That's not like Peter at all. I saw you two boys talking to him after the game, so I thought he might have said something to you."

"He did tell us about his grandfather, who was supposed to have visited today," Frank said. "Do you think he was upset about that?"

"His grandfather called," the worried woman replied. "He told us he wouldn't be able to make the trip. I knew Peter would be disappointed, but not enough to leave the house like that."

"I'm sorry," Frank said, "but he only told us that he was going home to wait for his grandfather's call. I have a hunch, though, where he might be. I'll check it out."

Frank hung up the receiver. "Come on," he told his brother, "we're going to the gym."

On their way to Bayport High, where the game had been played earlier that day, Frank recounted his telephone conversation to Joe. They knew from past experience that Peter liked to practice shooting baskets in his spare time, and might well have gone there if he was troubled about something.

"Wait a minute," Joe objected. "The gym's closed by now."

"Not tonight," Frank said. "There's a dance going on in the cafeteria next to it."

The tall boy was indeed there, practicing all by himself in the empty gymnasium.

"Hey, Peter!" Joe called out as they walked through the door.

Peter stopped and wheeled around to face his schoolmates. "What are you guys doing here?" he asked in a less than friendly manner.

"Oh, come on, Peter!" Joe sighed at his friend's hostile tone. "Your mother's worried about you. She called us, hoping we'd know where you were."

"Well, I guess you found me." The basketball star shrugged, his manner softening.

"Why don't you tell us what's bothering you?" Frank asked, as he picked the ball off the court and made a short jump shot. "We suspect there's more to your story than you told us at the game."

A moment of silence followed, while Peter considered how much to confide in his teammates.

"I want to show you something," he said at last, motioning with his hand and leading the way into the locker room.

Frank and Joe followed him to his locker. He opened it and withdrew a shoe box. "Get a load of this," he said and opened the carton.

A dead bird lay inside!

"This was sent to me from New Orleans," Peter went on. "There was a note in the bird's mouth with my grandfather's name written on it nine times!"

"Sounds like witchcraft of some kind," Joe commented.

"Voodoo," the basketball star said. "I looked it up. It's supposed to produce a spell for the purpose of hurting an enemy."

Frank looked questioningly at Peter. "Your grandfather lives in New Orleans, so you suspect he is somehow mixed up with this?"

"Exactly." The boy nodded. "When he called tonight, I didn't mention the bird 'cause I didn't want him to worry about it. He sounded a little tense, and I'm convinced that he was hiding something from me, something he was afraid to tell me."

Peter's face clouded over again as he put the box containing the dead bird back in his locker. "Please don't let my mom know about this," he pleaded. "To think Grandpa was mixed up with some kind of voodoo cult would drive her nuts. That's why I came here tonight. I was too upset to sit around home with a poker face and not say anything."

Frank and Joe agreed to keep Peter's secret if he agreed to return home. Then they switched off the gymnasium lights and got in their cars.

"Maybe we should take a trip south," Joe said, once they were back on the road. "I'd sure like to follow up on that lead Gloria, the snake charmer, gave us. The old man she told us about fits our clues like a glove. We could also check up on Peter's grandad and see if there is really something to that voodoo stuff."

Frank threw a sidelong glance at his younger brother. "Georgia is a long way from New Orleans, Louisiana," he informed Joe. "And we're a long way from either place. How do you suggest we get there?"

The blond youth sank into his seat. "I don't know, but if we don't go, we might never get to the bottom of this mystery!"

At home, they told their father the latest news.

"It certainly sounds as if the old man that snake charmer described to you is someone we ought to investigate," Mr. Hardy told his sons. "He could be the man you saw at McPhee's, and the one who put those snakes in your car."

"And the fact that he works in flea markets fits into the picture, too," Frank said. "Maybe that's how he sells whatever he steals. He probably doesn't make much money on it, but unless he's got a reliable fence, a flea market certainly would be a good place to get rid of his booty."

"You know what bothers me?" Joe asked. "There's almost too much evidence. Everything fits so neatly that I have the feeling someone's trying to send us off on a wild-goose chase. Those clues practically jumped out and bit us!" he concluded with a grin, unable to resist the pun.

"Could be," Mr. Hardy agreed. "If that's the case, though, I think we'd best play along for a while and see what happens."

"Does that mean we can go to Swamp Creek to check out the guy?" Frank asked excitedly.

"I think it would be a good idea," his father replied. "Are you up to it?"

"Are we!" the boys cried in unison. "I'll call the airport right away!"

"Why don't we ask Chet if he wants to come along?" Joe suggested. "He might be of help."

"Good idea," Frank said and dialed Chet's number.

Their friend had saved money over the winter just for this kind of trip, and was eager to join the Hardys in unraveling the mystery.

"I'll make reservations and let you know what time we'll have to leave," Frank said, and hung up. Then he called the airport. He was able to book them on an afternoon flight to Savannah the next day, and notified Chet so he would be ready when the Hardys came to pick him up.

"And now I'd better talk to Peter," he said. "After we finish in Swamp Creek, we'll be able to go to visit his grandfather, too. Right, Dad?"

"I don't see why not," Mr. Hardy replied.

Frank dialed the Walkers' number. His friend was still up and answered the phone.

"Hello, Peter?" Frank said. "We're following a case to Georgia tomorrow and if we solve it there, we can go to New Orleans."

"You mean you could find out whether Grandpa is really mixed up with voodoo?" Peter asked excitedly.

"Perhaps," Frank replied. "And if we do, we want to know how to get hold of him."

"His club is called Stretch's," Peter told him. "He named it after himself. It's right on Bourbon Street in the heart of the dixieland jazz club district. He's got an apartment upstairs with extra bedrooms and can easily put you up."

"Thanks," Frank said.

"I hope you can go," Peter said. "Besides, it's Mardi Gras time there. You'd enjoy it."

"That's right!" the young detective exclaimed with a laugh, referring to the yearly festival that transformed the whole city into one big party for a week. "I've always wanted to go to Mardi Gras, but I doubt we'll have much time for partying, even if we get there."

He concluded the conversation, then the brothers went upstairs to bed. The following day, Mr. Hardy gave his sons a list of items stolen from the

45

various galleries, and after lunch, they picked up Chet and drove to the airport.

The plane made only one stop, in Washington, D.C., before continuing south to Savannah, an old and handsome port on the Atlantic Ocean. It had been nicknamed "The Queen of the Georgia Coast" more than a hundred years ago, when it thrived as the center for the South's cotton trade.

"It's like being in another century," Chet said as they walked down the old city's streets to the bus station.

Frank smiled. "This whole case seems like it's from another century. So we're in the right place."

The boys boarded a bus leading south. Night had fallen by the time they got off in the little town called Swamp Creek.

There were several stores and a motel along its main street, but the stores were closed and there wasn't a soul around. Long strands of Spanish moss hung from cypress trees lining the street, giving it an eerie appearance.

With their luggage in hand, the boys went to the motel to check in for the night. It was called the Swamp Creek Inn, and its name was written in flashing red neon lights outside the lobby.

"Does anybody live around here?" Chet asked the clerk, relieved to see a human face. "It seems so deserted."

The clerk, a balding man who was even heavier than Chet, was slow to answer the visitors. "Everybody's home having dinner," he said at last in a soft southern drawl. "Your room is number sixteen, the one down at the end." He handed Chet a key.

"Speaking of dinner," Frank said, "is there somewhere to eat near here?"

The clerk motioned with his thumb to a door in the back of the lobby. "Restaurant's open," he said.

After they had dropped off their luggage, Chet led the way to the restaurant. It was filled with tables and chairs, but no people. Uncertain, the boys stopped at the door, wondering whether to take seats or leave.

"May I help you?" asked a girl dressed in a white waitress outfit. She was pretty, with long, light brown hair and big blue eyes. Chet liked her melodic accent.

"Are you open for dinner?" Joe inquired.

"We are," the girl replied, then showed them to a table and gave them menus. "Are you here for the roundup?" she asked once they were seated.

"The roundup?" Frank looked puzzled.

"The rattlesnake roundup," the waitress told them. "It starts tomorrow."

Realizing that the boys had no idea what she was talking about, she explained that the next day was the beginning of Swamp Creek's annual rattlesnake festival, when people came from all over to help capture rattlesnakes.

"Why would they want to do that?" Chet asked.

"Oh, it's a big event," the young waitress said in a serious tone. "Every year we catch the snakes as they come out of hibernation. They're easiest to get then because they all hibernate together in dens. By catching them, we can keep their numbers way down." The girl made a sweeping gesture around the empty room. "By tomorrow, this place will be full of people who are coming for the roundup. I just thought you were the first to get here."

"No, we're here on an investigation," Chet told the girl, trying to impress her. "We have more important things to do than catch rattlers."

The waitress's eyes widened. "Are you guys FBI agents or something?"

"Not exactly." Frank chuckled. "But we're looking for someone." He opened his suitcase and withdrew the burlap sack with the rattlesnake emblem printed on it. "Have you ever seen something like this around here?" he asked the girl, holding the sack up.

"Sure," she replied. "Rattlesnake Clem uses those things. That's one of his bags."

"Tell us about him!" Joe urged.

"Is he the man you're looking for?" she asked in surprise.

"Maybe," Frank told her. "Do you know where we can find him?"

"Clem lives on Hull Street. His full name is Clemson Marion. But he's rarely home. What do you want with him?"

"Oh, we just want to ask him a few questions," Joe said vaguely. "Can you tell us how we can get in touch with him?"

"Wait a minute." The girl hurried from the room and returned a moment later with the motel clerk. He scratched his head in wonder as he approached the boys.

"My niece Sadie tells me that you're looking for Rattlesnake Clem," he said, pulling up a chair. "What do you want with him?"

"We need some information from him," Frank said in a matter-of-fact voice. "We're private detectives."

The clerk looked at them for a moment, then said, "He'll probably be at the roundup tomorrow. He has a place on Hull Street, but he's never there. He usually comes to the festivities to cause trouble." Noticing the question in the boys' faces, he went on to explain that Clem was a rattlesnake lover. He felt the roundups, in which thousands of the creatures were killed every year, were evil and should be stopped, so he kept trying to disrupt them.

"He's an ornery old guy," the clerk concluded. "Don't ever get on the bad side of him, unless you want a rattlesnake dropped down the back of your shirt."

The pretty, blue-eyed waitress brought the boys a hot meal of steak, corn, and hush puppies. When they were finished, they thanked her and her uncle for the information, then went to their room. It contained only two beds, so Joe volunteered to sleep on a cot provided by the clerk.

"I've read about rattlesnake roundups," Frank said after they had settled down and turned off the light. "They're not really held because people are worried about too many rattlesnakes. That's just an excuse to have a festival so a town can raise money."

"Seems like a good idea," Chet observed. "It'll fill up the motel and restaurant with paying customers. This place could use the cash."

"But at the same time, it'll cost hundreds of rattlesnakes their lives," Joe said from his cot.

Conversation stopped as the boys drifted off to sleep, vaguely wondering what an old man living near the Okefenokee Swamp might have to do with the recent burglaries. They woke in the morning from noises in the street.

Joe went to the window and pulled back the curtains. "Hey, look at this!" he called out to Frank and Chet.

5 Rattlesnake Roundup

Swamp Creek's main street, which had been empty the night before, was completely flooded with people who had arrived to participate in the round-up. Many were carrying sticks and bags. Between two telephone poles, a huge banner read: WEL-COME TO SWAMP CREEK'S ANNUAL RATTLESNAKE ROUNDUP.

"They sure are ready to get on with it," Frank said, peering out the window over Joe's shoulder.

"Well, I'm ready, too," Joe declared.

The three boys put on their clothes and went outside into the morning sun. After a quick break-fast, they were soon among the throng of snake hunters gathering in the center of town.

A platform was set up outside the general store.

Several men stood on it, wearing big straw hats with rattlesnake skins wrapped around the tops.

"They must be managing the event," Joe commented as the boys worked their way through the crowd toward the platform.

Just then, one of the men announced that the hunters would be divided into several parties, each with a group leader.

Once the throng had been split up, Frank asked one of the straw-hatted men which of the groups would be going toward the swamp.

"Mine is," he replied and motioned for the boys to join him. He was a small, wiry-looking man with deep-set eyes. "I'm Billy," he introduced himself to his party. "How many of you have been to a roundup before?"

Most hands went up, and the leader seemed pleased. "Well, I guess I won't have to explain it to you, then," he went on. "For those who haven't done this, just hang back and watch. You'll catch on pretty quick."

"I'll hang back all right," Chet mumbled to his friends. "*Way* back!"

With the group leader in front, the snake hunters walked down the main street. In time, they moved off the road and into the woods that bordered the swamp.

"This here's the Okefenokee Swamp," Billy told

his followers and gestured toward the dense tangle of bushes, cypress trees, and watery bog to his left. "About forty different species of snakes live in there, from coral snakes to water moccasins to rattlers. What we're lookin' for today, though, is the Eastern Diamondback rattler."

"Why only the Eastern Diamondback?" one member of the group asked.

" 'Cause they're the easiest to catch," Billy said with a wink. "But if anyone here wants to go diving for water moccasins, I'm positive it would be appreciated." The wiry man paused for a moment to make sure everyone got his little joke, then he led the group further into the woods.

Some time later, he stopped again. "Ought to be a whole nest of 'em here," he said, pointing to a rocky hill.

They approached the hill slowly. At first, it appeared to be clear of any snakes. But as they drew closer, signs of movement were visible between the rocks.

Chet gasped. "The place is just crawling with them!"

Hundreds of snakes seemed to fill the cracks and crevices in the rocky mound. They were clearly Eastern Diamondbacks, marked by the diamond-shaped patterns on their bodies, and they moved slowly if at all. Most were coiled and silent, taking in the sun after several months of hibernation.

The hunters started to catch the lazy diamond-backs with their sticks that were forked at the end. By pinning the snakes' heads with the forked part, the men were able to grab them by the back of the neck and throw them into their bags.

The boys watched with fascination. Obviously, the crowd was enjoying the sport, but Frank, Joe, and Chet did not join in.

Suddenly, out of the sky, a large rattlesnake plopped to the ground just a few feet from where Joe stood!

"Hey, what's going on?" he shouted as he jumped back.

Frank and Chet retreated as well when a couple more rattlers hit the ground near them.

"They're falling out of the trees!" a man cried as panic seized the group. "Somebody must be throwing them!"

As Frank dodged another rattler, everyone looked up in terror, searching the trees for the source of the falling serpents.

"Ha-ha-ha-ha-ha!" A laughing voice suddenly bellowed from above. "You folks are real brave, all right! Ha-ha-ha-ha!"

Sitting high on the limb of a thick tree sat an old man in a tricornered hat! He held a sack full of snakes, which he flung one by one upon the startled group.

"That must be Rattlesnake Clem!" Chet cried.

"Tricornered hat and all," Joe put in, stepping away from the tree.

The old man's expression turned severe as the hunters below gazed up at him in fright and backed away.

"Now skidaddle!" he shouted harshly. "And if I see you all out here huntin' again, I won't miss you when I throw 'em!"

"I'll see that you're arrested for this, Clem!" the group leader called out angrily.

"You go ahead and do that," Rattlesnake Clem called back.

With that, the old man let go of his sack and grabbed a rope he had tied to the tree limb. The other end was attached to another tree, and he slid to the ground some distance from the hunters. The Hardys didn't even try chasing him as he disappeared into the swamp, but Joe picked up the sack.

"We don't have a chance of catching him," he grumbled. "He knows that swamp and we don't. We'd just be bargaining for trouble."

Frank nodded. Not too long afterward, the group returned to Swamp Creek and disbanded. After the encounter with Clem, the hunters' excitement over bagging snakes had lessened.

The Hardys and Chet followed Billy to the county police station, where he planned to make a formal complaint against Clem.

The sheriff sat behind his desk eating a candy bar. He was broad-shouldered, but a bit too heavy around the middle to be in excellent physical condition.

"What can I do for you, Billy?" he asked as he finished the candy bar and tossed the wrapper into a wastebasket.

The group leader explained what Clem had done, and a slight grin played around the sheriff's lips. "So old Clem is at it again," he said. "Sounds like he's just getting more and more ornery as the years go by."

"That's putting it mildly!" Billy growled. "Someone could've been bitten. You ought to find him and lock him up!"

"I'll talk to him," the county sheriff replied more seriously. "You're right, this'll have to stop."

Frank stepped up to the desk. "We'd like to have a chance to speak with him, too," he said and explained their reasons for wanting to question Clem.

A surprised look came over the sheriff's face as he listened to Frank's story. "You think that old Clem is responsible for a bunch of burglaries in other states?" he asked in disbelief.

"Do you know where he's been in the past two or three weeks?" Frank countered with a question of his own.

"Well, no," the broad-shouldered man replied. "But old Clem, he's just a crazy guy who tries to protect the wildlife, although I admit he has some strange methods of doing it."

Frank shrugged. "I know he doesn't fit the professional thief type, but there's just too much evidence to ignore."

"Look at this," Joe told the sheriff, presenting the two burlap sacks and laying them on the desk. "We found one of these outside a burglarized antique shop in Bayport. Clem dropped the other one before he left the tree this morning."

The sheriff studied the bags bearing exactly the same picture of the coiled rattlesnake and the "Don't Tread on Me" inscription. "I see what you mean," he said, looking thoughtfully at the youths. Then he sighed. "I expect Clem will be around tomorrow. I won't do anything until you've had a chance to talk to him. Try his house early in the morning. You should be able to catch him then."

The boys thanked the sheriff and left the police station. When they returned to the center of Swamp Creek, they saw that many of the hunters

57

had finished for the day. A fenced-in pit had been dug in an empty lot behind the general store, and hundreds of captured rattlers now swarmed inside.

"I wonder what they plan to do with them." Chet shuddered as he stared into the pit.

"They'll probably destroy most of them," Frank said. "Some might be bought by zoos or collectors. Others'll be used for science."

By now, the trio was getting hungry, so they went back to the motel for dinner. As the waitress had said, the restaurant was full of rattlesnake hunters. There was even a local bluegrass band for entertainment. The boys took a table and listened to the music.

"This is more like it," Chet said, happy to be sitting and listening to the band. "Now all I want is something to eat."

"Hi, guys," Sadie greeted them when she got to their table. "Ready for dinner?"

"Sure." Chet grinned. "I'm starved. What's the special?"

"We're only serving one thing today." She giggled.

"What's that?"

"Barbecued rattlesnake!"

Chet's smile dropped from his face. "That's all? Barbecued rattlesnake?"

"Come on, Chet," Joe encouraged him. "Everybody else is eating it."

The plump boy looked glumly around him at the plates of other customers, half expecting to see rattlers coiled up on them with sprigs of parsley in the middle. Instead, he saw tasty-looking round chunks of meat covered with sauce. It smelled good, too.

"I'll try it," he said at last. "But I won't promise I'll like it."

Sadie brought them each a plate. Chet grumbled about it, but he still managed to put away a second helping.

"Let's go back to the room," Frank said, once the meal was over. "I want to call Dad."

Stuffed from the delicious dinner, the boys walked to Room 16. Chet opened the door and flopped down on his bed before turning on the light. Just as he hit, the silence in the room was broken by a loud rattling sound.

"Eeeeeeee!" Chet screamed in pain as the sharp fangs of an Eastern Diamondback rattler dug into his leg!

6 *Poison Scare*

Joe flipped on the light switch.

"It got me!" Chet cried, springing away from the rattlesnake, which was preparing for another strike.

"Outside, quick!" Frank ordered.

The chubby boy hobbled to the door of their room, where Frank and Joe cradled him under his arms and hurried him out. By the time they reached the lobby, Chet's leg was already swelling and hurting.

"We need to get him to a doctor fast," Joe told the clerk.

The man inspected Chet's leg and let out a low whistle. "Looks bad," he commented. "Put him in my car. It's the blue Chevy out front."

Chet groaned with pain as Frank and Joe carried him outside. A few seconds later, the clerk came to the car holding some implements in his hand. The young waitress was right behind him.

"You drive," he told Joe, throwing him the keys.

Frank and Joe climbed into the front seat, while the clerk and Sadie helped Chet into the back. The clerk gave Joe directions to the local doctor's office as they went along. At the same time, he applied a tourniquet to Chet's leg above the snake bite to reduce circulation of the blood. Sadie held Chet's head on her lap, and mopped his feverish forehead with a handkerchief.

Once at the doctor's, they lifted Chet from the car and took him inside. The doctor was a thin, graying man who wore glasses. He had Frank and Joe set Chet on his examination table.

"Does this hurt?" he asked Chet, pressing gently down on the bitten area.

"Yowwwww!" Chet exclaimed. "It sure does."

"That's good," the doctor told him. "It would be numb if the bite were severe."

He checked Chet for tingling around the mouth and yellowed vision, as well as signs of the bite's severity. Then he made an antiseptic wet dressing for the bite and gave Chet a shot of antivenom.

"He ought to be up and around in a day or two," the doctor announced once he was finished. "I usually get a couple of bite victims during these roundups, so I keep plenty of medicine on hand."

The Hardys heaved a sigh of relief. "So he'll be okay?" Joe said.

"Just keep him quiet and rested," the doctor replied. "The swelling should be down by morning. And from now on, do yourselves a favor and stay away from those critters."

When they got to the Swamp Creek Inn, the clerk, whose name turned out to be Al, helped the boys capture the snake in their room. Then they carried Chet in and laid him on his bed.

"Boy, you're heavy," Frank kidded him as they put him down.

"Well, excuuuuuse me!" the chubby boy replied indignantly, now in good enough spirits to participate in the banter. "I'm sorry I didn't check the bed for rattlesnakes. Next time I'll be more careful."

Frank and Joe smiled at their friend before continuing in a more serious tone.

"I bet Clem was behind this," Joe said as he sat down on the edge of his cot.

"It seems like it," Frank said angrily. "Unless the snake crawled through the window on its own."

"If Clem did it, it means he's not just playing scare games anymore," Joe went on. "That diamondback is a lot more deadly than the pygmy rattlers we found in our car."

"Why don't you go to the police and have him locked up?" Chet blurted. "The guy tried to kill me!"

"Because we can't prove anything at this point," Joe said.

"I'll call Dad first thing in the morning," Frank decided. "He may have uncovered something since we left."

As soon as he woke up the next day, he reached for the phone and dialed the Hardy number. Aunt Gertrude answered, and after telling her what had happened so far, Frank asked to talk to his father.

"It's bad enough that you go off and risk your own lives," Aunt Gertrude said sternly before turning the phone over to Mr. Hardy. "But don't make your friend Chet the victim of your shenanigans. Poor boy!"

Frank began to explain, but his aunt had already given the phone to his father. The famous detective listened with interest, happy to hear that they had tracked down the man in the tricornered hat. Then he said, "Even the fact that Clem is known to be away from home a lot fits into the picture."

"Have any other art galleries or antique shops been robbed since we left town?" Joe queried.

"None that fit the mold of this particular string," Fenton Hardy replied.

63

"Then if we can learn how Clem makes his trips, we'll have a case on him. Right?"

"That's right," Mr. Hardy answered. "I'll check with Savannah airport and see if he's been flying in and out lately. You investigate the private airports, okay?"

"Will do." Frank hung up the phone and looked at his brother. "We'll have to find out if there are any private airports in the area," he said.

Joe's puzzled expression was interrupted by a knock on the door. He opened it to let in the waitress.

She carried a book under her arm and went straight to Chet's bed to see how he was doing.

"I brought you something to read," the pretty blue-eyed girl told him, her melodic southern accent ringing cheerily. "It's all about snakes. I thought you'd like to know about them since one just bit you."

Chet, who had by now developed a crush on Sadie, took the book and promised to read the whole thing. He then groaned theatrically, trying to play on her sympathy for his condition.

"Sadie—" Frank chuckled, finally interrupting his friend's antics. "Is there an airport nearby that handles private planes?"

"Yes," the girl replied brightly. "Just north of

here. Does it have something to do with your mystery?"

Frank told her it might, then asked her if she could drive them there.

"I'd love to!" she said, excited to help with their investigation.

Chet emitted a low growl, mad at his friends for leaving him and taking the girl of his dreams with them. Before they drove off, he made Sadie promise to check up on him as soon as she returned.

At the airport, a small operation located a few miles from Swamp Creek, the sleuths questioned the manager about recent flights of Clemson Marion. There weren't any.

"Did anyone go to or come from Bayport in the last few days?" Frank pressed on.

"Bayport. Matter of fact, yes. A blue Cessna flew in from there two days ago. It's still here. The pilot registered himself as Roger Mann. He came in last week, too, but went back to Bayport the same day."

"What does he look like?" Frank inquired.

"Don't know. He was wearing sunglasses and a hat, almost as if he didn't want anyone to recognize him."

Joe snapped his fingers. "I bet it was Clem!"

"Was he an older man?" Frank went on, doubting Joe's hasty conclusion.

The manager shook his head, and Joe's hopes for a quick verdict on Clem fell. Clem was in his sixties!

"Wait a minute," the manager said, seeing the boys' disappointment. "The pilot wasn't old, but he had a passenger with him whom I never saw except at a distance. He could have been an old guy, the one you're looking for."

"Did he also hide his identity?" Frank queried, trying not to get his hopes up again.

"Maybe." The manager shrugged. "I don't know if he kept away from me on purpose, but anyway, I didn't get to see him."

"I'd like to take a look inside that plane," Joe spoke up.

"Can't let you do that," the manager told him. "You'd have to get permission from the pilot, and he didn't say where he was staying. Sorry."

Frank and Joe asked the man to contact them at the Swamp Creek Inn if and when the Cessna's pilot and passenger reappeared, then they returned to the motel with Sadie and checked the register for Roger Mann. He was not listed, nor did any of the townfolk they asked know him.

"If he's involved in our case, he's probably using different names," Frank commented as they went back to their room. "And with all the strangers in town for the roundup, it would be difficult to single him out."

In the motel room, Frank telephoned Mr. Hardy again, who reported that Clem had not flown in and out of Savannah in the past year. Frank told him about the blue Cessna and Roger Mann, and gave his father the plane's license number. Mr. Hardy promised to have Sam Radley, his operative, check into it.

"By the way," the detective said before hanging up, "your friend Peter Walker phoned. He wanted to know whether you were going to New Orleans."

"We're planning on it, Dad, but we can't promise him when we'll be able to go. First, we have to get to the bottom of this mystery here."

"Right. And good luck!"

Frank hung up and turned his attention to Chet. "How're you doing, old buddy?"

"I've been reading this book Sadie gave me," Chet said. "It has a chapter in it about voodoo. Voodoo!" Chet repeated in a ghostly tone. "Just the sound of it gives me the creeps!"

7 A Frightening Ritual

"What does the book say about voodoo?" Frank asked Chet.

"It says that voodoo, a form of black magic, originally came from the African worship of serpents," his friend replied, sitting up in bed. "Now voodoo is only practiced in Haiti, where snakes even live in the rafters of people's homes."

"Haiti," Frank said softly, musing over the Caribbean island located south of Florida and just east of Cuba. "Don't they speak a dialect of French down there called Creole?"

Joe's eyes lit up as he realized what his brother was getting at. "That's right!" he replied. "And the Creole dialect is also spoken in New Orleans. Maybe voodoo is practiced there as well!"

"So Peter's suspicion could be on the mark after all," Frank stated. "His grandfather might really be mixed up with a voodoo cult!"

"I think we should stay away from any place where people have something to do with black magic!" Chet declared. "You know what they do if they want to get rid of you? They steal a piece of your clothing, make a doll out of it that represents you, and stick a pin into it. Then you get sick and die!"

"Come on, Chet, you don't really believe that, do you?" Joe teased his friend.

"From what I read, it's worked for the Haitians for centuries," Chet mumbled. "At least *they* think it did. And that's good enough for me!"

"Hold on," Frank said, breaking into a grin. "I think you're letting your imagination run away with itself. Let's stick to one snake cult at a time and visit old Clem."

Chet's swollen leg was nearly back to its normal size, but it would be another day before he could walk on it. Frank and Joe left him in bed and headed on foot to Hull Street, which turned out to be on the far end of town.

They asked a passerby where Clem's house was, and were directed to a small cottage almost hidden by trees.

"I hope he won't mind us paying him a visit," Frank said, as they made their way through the tangle of bushes into the front yard. It was littered with junk. Next to the open garage stood an old, rusty plow, a bathtub with legs, and an ancient wood-burning stove. It was sprayed with primer.

"I suppose he's fixing it up so he can sell it as an antique," Joe said, pointing to the stove.

Frank nodded. "What I would like to see is a sign of life around here," he muttered. "Well, let's try the door."

The bell did not work, so the boys knocked. They heard a rustle inside the house, but no one came out to admit them. Frank knocked again and again. After a few minutes, they heard footsteps, and a grumpy voice called out, "Who's there?"

"Frank and Joe Hardy," Frank replied. "We'd like to talk to you for a few minutes, please."

"What about?"

"Rattlesnakes!"

"Oh, sure, I'll be right there," Clem replied in a friendly tone.

"His favorite subject changed his mood instantly," Joe whispered. "I wonder—"

The door opened and the wizened old man clad in overalls and a turtleneck sweater came out. The smile he had on his face disappeared as soon as he saw the two boys.

"What do you want?" he demanded gruffly.

"We came from Bayport and we'd like to know what you were doing there two days ago," Frank said.

"At McPhee's Antiques," Joe added.

The grizzled man made no reply, but looked genuinely puzzled. Then he squinted at the Hardys. "You want to talk about rattlesnakes, eh? Well, come in. I'll show 'em to you."

He led the way through his simply furnished cottage and out into the backyard. In a rough wooden shed were about a dozen cages containing various kinds of rattlers, including diamondbacks and pygmies.

"These are my pets," Clem said. "They tell me whether people are honest or not." A sly grin appeared on his lips as he opened a cage and took out two large diamondbacks. He handed one to each of the boys.

"Here, play with them a little!" He cackled. "Go ahead, take 'em!"

Uneasily, both boys grabbed the snakes as they had seen the hunters do the day before—behind the back of the head. But disapproval registered on Clem's face.

"Not that way!" he corrected. "Like this!"

He took a third snake from the cage and held it by its body, stroked it, and lifted it over his head. Then he returned it to the cage.

Frank and Joe exchanged a glance, then handled their snakes as Clem had done. It was their only chance to get the old man to talk, they realized.

"Nice little snakie," Joe crooned. "I always wanted to pet one of you. There, that's good. Nice snake—"

"Okay," Clem said, apparently satisfied. "You can give them to me now." He took the two rattlers and put them back in their cage.

Frank discreetly wiped the perspiration from his forehead. "Ah—now can we talk?"

"Come inside the house." Clem led them into his cottage and offered them chairs in the small kitchen.

"I thought the King had sent ya," he said when they were all seated. "Guess I was wrong."

"Who's the King?" Frank asked.

"Why, King George the Third," Clem said with a twinkle in his eye. "The King of England and my arch enemy." With this, he took his tricornered hat from a peg and placed it on his head. "I'll tell you about him," he added.

Sitting in his kitchen, Rattlesnake Clem seemed to be quite different from what the boys had seen before. His suspicious nature had left him and a faraway look clouded his eyes as he began his story.

"You see," Clem told them, "I'm the great-great-grandson of Francis Marion, better known as the

Swamp Fox. That's why I wear this tricornered hat."

"And that Revolutionary War emblem on your rattlesnake bags?" Joe asked.

Clem nodded. "That's right. My great-great-grandpappy used to camp out in the swamps with his band of soldiers. He hid by day and attacked the British outposts by night. That's how he got the name 'Swamp Fox.'"

"And you've decided to take after him, even though the Revolutionary War was finished more than two hundred years ago," Frank said with a hint of challenge in his voice.

"But the war ain't over yet," the old man said craftily.

Frank and Joe glanced at each other, aware that Clem was either crazy or doing a good job of pretending he was.

"The war ain't over because King George the Third of England still lives," Clem went on with a gleam in his eye. "And he's out there taxing the tea off the colonies. It's my job to put a stop to it!"

The Hardys knew that George the Third had been the King of England when the American Revolution broke out. Many of the early settlers hated him for levying heavy taxes on their goods, and this taxation had been the cause for the Revolution. But that was over two centuries ago!

"What makes you think King George is still alive?" Frank asked.

"I seen him!" Clem answered in a shout. "He came out of the swamp just to tax the colonies. He ain't dead, that's for sure. He's just been hidin' all these years."

Seeing that he was getting nowhere with Clem's strange tale of the long dead King of England, Frank questioned him about the Bayport burglary and the rattlesnake that had been planted in Chet's bed.

"I ain't never even heard of your Bayport!" the grizzled old man said hotly. "So how could I be there stealin' stuff? I can't tell you how one of my snake sacks got up there, and I can't say who was wearin' that tricornered hat. Only it weren't me!"

"Listen," Joe said, getting to his feet and clenching his hands into fists. "We almost have enough on you to go to the police right now. So you'd better come clean."

Clem stood up himself, anger flashing across his face. "Listen, sonny, don't you try and threaten me! I told you I ain't never been to Bayport and I ain't a liar!"

Having made his point, Clem sat back down. "I admit I dropped that rattler in your bed," he told them in a calmer tone. "I heard you'd come around here asking questions about me and I figured I'd give you a little scare. Sorry about your friend, but I didn't think one of you was gonna lie down on top of the critter."

"You put the snake in Chet's bed just because you heard we were looking for you?" Frank asked in disbelief.

"Thought you were agents for the King," Clem explained. "He knows that I'm out to get him, and he's gonna get me first if he can. That's why I made you boys handle the snakes. If you were the King's agents, you'd have been too yellow-bellied to do it."

Realizing that they were getting nothing out of this modern day Swamp Fox, the Hardys said good-bye and left.

"Either he's been inhaling too much swamp gas or he's trying to play crazy with us," Joe remarked with a shrug as they followed the road back to town. "That King George story is the craziest thing I've ever heard."

"We'll just have to dig up the plane's pilot, Roger Mann." Frank sighed.

A half-hour later, the boys were back on Swamp Creek's main street.

"Look!" Frank exclaimed as they approached the motel. "The sheriff's car!"

8 *Lost in the Swamp*

Parked in front of their motel room was a police car bearing the county sheriff's insignia, a large gold star on its side. The boys quickened their pace, worried that Chet had been the victim of another attack.

They opened the door and heaved a sigh of relief when they saw Chet sitting up in bed, apparently all right.

The sheriff was standing next to the window, which had been shattered. Broken glass covered the floor near it. "Hi, fellows," he said. "Your friend here called me when this happened. Somebody threw a rock through your window. It had a note attached to it."

The sheriff handed a crumpled piece of paper to

Frank and Joe. It had the coiled rattlesnake and the "Don't Tread on Me" inscription stamped on the top. Below, written in script, was:

MEET ME IN THE SWAMP AT SUNSET.
ASK RICK DOUGLAS TO TAKE YOU THERE.
CLEM

"Wait a minute," Frank said. "We were with Clem this morning. He couldn't have thrown this note in here."

"Maybe he beat you back here," the sheriff told them. "It happened less than five minutes ago."

"Who's Rick Douglas?" Joe queried.

"Ricky runs an airboat operation," the sheriff informed them. "He's a boy about your age. Knows the Okefenokee Swamp inside out. He hires out to take tourists sightseeing.

"Where can we find him?" Frank asked.

"Just take the same road you used to get to Clem's, but go a half mile farther, then turn left into the swamp. There are signs."

"I saw them on the way back here," Joe said, referring to a couple of markers indicating the way to the Okefenokee Swamp boat tours. "Let's go."

"Let me know what you find out," the sheriff said. "Tell Clem he'll have to pay for that broken window and that I want to talk with him anyway."

The sleuths left the room and followed the route

to Clem's place. They followed the signs leading to the tours and finally found themselves at a dock at the edge of the swamp.

Tied to the dock was a long, flat airboat with a huge fan mounted on the back end. The fan was used to propel the boat over very shallow waters that a normal outboard motorboat would have been unable to navigate.

"Are you the Hardys?" asked a slender boy who emerged from a cabin next to the dock.

"Yes, and you must be Rick." Frank greeted him. "We had a note from Clem. He said you'd take us to meet him."

Rick nodded. "He wants to see you about something. Acted like it was real important. I'm supposed to bring you out there."

Frank and Joe climbed into the passenger seats in front of the craft, while Rick sat further back where he could operate the huge fan.

"How far are we going?" Frank asked over the loud hum of the fan as they eased away from the dock.

"It's quite a distance," the boy called back. "The Okefenokee Swamp is a mighty big place."

From the waitress, the Hardys had learned about the swamp. It was a national park that covered seventy square miles of southeastern Georgia and

northern Florida. The Suwannee River ran through the middle of it, but the rest was nearly all swampland. It was inhabited mostly by snakes, birds, and alligators.

Skimming the surface of the water, Rick maneuvered his craft over marshes and bogs. The airboat even glided over mud flats and exposed sand bars with the ease of a car cruising down a smooth street.

"This is it," he finally declared and pulled up to a level of higher ground covered with trees. "Clem wants you to meet him in a shack behind those trees. I'll wait for you here."

"Thanks," Frank said and the Hardys hopped off. They walked into the thicket of trees, expecting to come upon a shack. But there was no sign of human habitation anywhere!

"Hey, there's nothing here," Joe said, looking around him. "Rick must've picked the wrong place."

Just then, the young detectives heard the sound of the airboat's engines starting up.

"He's leaving!" Joe shouted in alarm and they ran from among the trees toward the boat.

Their hearts sank as they watched the boat disappear into the swamp, zooming over the water. Apparently, it had all been a setup to drop them in the middle of nowhere and leave them there!

"That creep!" Joe shouted angrily after the boy. "Wait until I get back. I'll make that punk and his airboat one big pile of rubbish!"

"The question is," Frank said with a sinking feeling in the pit of his stomach, "how do we get back? We must be ten miles into the swamp!"

The sun was already near the horizon. In a few more minutes, it would be dark.

"We'd better prepare to spend the night," Joe decided, watching the sun disappear. "We should be able to make it out of here, but not without light."

"I won't argue with you." Frank grunted. "I have no interest in swimming with alligators in the dark."

The night turned out to be chilly. Luckily, the boys had some matches, and were able to build a fire from wood they collected. They huddled near it to keep themselves warm.

Frank finally began to doze off, lulled to sleep by the sounds of the crackling fire and the wind in the trees. Joe continued feeding wood into the fire through most of the night. He finally dozed off himself, however, and the small fire soon burned down to a smoldering pile of ashes.

Suddenly, a noise jolted him from his sleep. Joe's eyes opened in fear as he strained to listen, not sure whether it had been real or part of a dream.

81

"GRRRRrrr!"

Realizing that the growl was not only real but also growing closer, Joe grabbed his brother's arm. "Wake up!"

"What is it?" Frank asked, coming to his senses.

"I don't know," Joe whispered. "Listen!"

Rustling sounds were audible from within the underbrush and seemed to be circling the youths. Again a low growl could be heard in the darkness.

"It's a wildcat," Frank deduced. He picked up a piece of firewood and stirred the ashes.

"GRRRRRRRRR!" growled the big cat as the red-hot embers beneath the ashes were uncovered.

"He's coming closer!" Joe cried in a hoarse whisper.

Just then, a pair of bright eyes appeared between some bushes.

At the same moment, Frank batted the red embers with his stick, stirring up a large cloud of burning ashes. Growling in alarm this time, the dangerous animal fled back into the underbrush.

"Boy, am I glad he's gone!" Frank sighed in relief.

Joe nodded. "He seemed to be as hungry as I am."

The boys built the fire back up as fast as they could, and made sure to tend it throughout the night. At dawn, they set out to find the spot where the cat had been able to cross over to the island.

"Here it is!" Joe called out, pointing to a shallow area that linked the small island with a larger body of land.

Frank and Joe waded out into the shallows and crossed over the stretch of dry land. The water never went above their knees, and the hard clay bottom easily supported their weight.

"Hold on," Joe ordered as they neared the land. "Those guys don't look too friendly, either."

Frank looked in the direction Joe had turned. Half submerged in the water, two large alligators lazed in the morning sun. Only their heads and the top of their backs were visible.

Just then, one of them broke from the shore and swam slowly out toward the sleuths. The boys froze in their footsteps.

"Ever wrestled an alligator before?" Frank joked nervously.

"If that thing gets any closer, we're dead!" Joe croaked.

The alligator, however, paid no attention to the strange visitors and veered off into deeper water. Cautiously, Frank and Joe continued to the shore, circling widely around the other alligator to avoid drawing its attention.

The land turned out to be swampy, and they had to trudge knee-deep through muddy bogs for a while before they reached higher and drier ground.

"We're heading west," Joe observed, judging their direction by the location of the sun. "Swamp Creek should be to the north."

"I know," Frank said. "I hope this stretch of land will lead us to the Suwannee River, which runs north and south through the middle of the swamp. We should be able to follow it back toward town."

The brothers continued their journey west, but thick underbrush made the going slow. By the time Frank and Joe had reached the banks of the river, their clothes were nearly in rags from being torn by the bushes.

Joe gazed north, up the lazy, winding river. "It sure would be nice to have a boat," he said wearily.

"Well, we don't have one," Frank told him with a shrug. "It's probably about five miles to the edge of the swamp and another mile or two to Swamp Creek. We should be able to make it."

The blond youth groaned.

Following the river north turned out to be even tougher than getting to it. Much of the terrain was swampy, and the boys even had to swim across several deep stretches of water, keeping their eyes open for alligators, water snakes, and other swamp creatures. By the time they had gone only a mile or two, they were nearly covered with mud and soaking wet.

"I need a rest," Joe insisted at last, having gotten less sleep than Frank the night before.

The dark-haired sleuth agreed, and they sat down on a fallen tree at the edge of the water.

"This is much tougher than I thought," Frank admitted, watching a water moccasin slip silently from a rock and into the river in search of prey.

"Hey, look!" Joe exclaimed suddenly, pointing down the river. "A boat!"

Both Hardys jumped to their feet and peered south. In the distance, a medium-sized motorboat was approaching from downriver.

"I didn't want to get my hopes up." Frank grinned. "But this is just what I had prayed for."

The boys quickly climbed to the end of the fallen tree, which stuck out into the river. As the motorboat approached, they waved and shouted for it to pick them up.

It was occupied by an elderly couple, both of whom wore straw hats and brightly colored shirts. The sight of the two boys, ragged and covered with mud, caused them to hesitate. Frank and Joe waited anxiously as the couple discussed whether to leave them there or not. Moments later, they heaved a sigh of relief as the man finally pulled up to the log.

"How'd you boys get stuck way out here?" the

woman asked in a thick southern accent as they climbed aboard.

"We think it was someone's idea of a prank," Frank answered grimly.

"Doesn't seem very funny to me," the man said in a surprised tone. "By the way," he went on, "my name is Walter. This is my wife, Peg."

Frank extended his hand toward the man to shake it.

"EEEEE!" the woman shrieked, staring at the youth's arm.

Startled, Frank looked and saw that it had several long, black leeches stuck to it! Both boys frantically tore off their shirts and pants, finding more of the bloodsuckers on their legs and backs. They had been too tired and covered with mud to notice them earlier.

Once they had removed the leeches, with the help of some salt the couple luckily had with them, the boys redressed. Peg made sandwiches for them as the boat continued its trip up the river, and the couple listened in amazement as the boys told their story.

Walter and Peg moored the boat near Swamp Creek, then went to the motel to pick up clean clothes for the boys. When they returned, Chet was with them.

"Now that's what I call real southern hospitality!"

Joe beamed after he'd changed. "If there's anything we can do for you, just—"

"Oh, never mind about that," the woman said in her heavy southern accent. "I just hope y'all would do the same for us if we were stuck in a swamp up North."

The boys thanked the couple again, and then went with Chet to find the airboat operator who had caused all their trouble.

The boat was at the landing when they got there.

"Now we're going to deal with another brand of southern hospitality," Joe said angrily and threw open the door to the cabin.

When Rick saw them, his mouth dropped. "I—I—how did you guys get here?" he stammered, cowering with fear at what they might do to him.

Joe grabbed him by his shirtfront and pressed him up against the wall. "Give us some straight answers or we'll turn you over to the sheriff," he demanded hotly.

"He—he made me do it!" the boy pleaded. "Look at the note. It's over there."

Frank picked up a piece of paper from the table. Like the one they had received through their motel window, it had the Revolutionary War emblem with the coiled snake stamped on it. The note ordered Rick to take Frank and Joe deep into the swamp and leave them for the snakes and alligators. If Rick didn't cooperate, the Swamp Fox would strike him soon and without warning. The note was signed "Rattlesnake Clem."

"Let him go," Frank said to Joe after reading the message. "Clem's the one who should be locked up."

"He already is," Chet said. "The sheriff picked him up last night."

"On what charge?" Joe asked, astonished.

Chet grinned. "The Bayport burglary!"

9 Air Search

"Take us to the sheriff's office," Frank told the airboat operator. "It's the least you can do to make up for abandoning us in the swamp."

Rick's old Chevy was parked behind the shed. The boys piled in and were soon on their way through town to the county police station. Once there, they found Clem locked up in one of the two jail cells. The grizzled old swamp dweller looked like a wild animal in a cage, pacing back and forth from one end to the other.

"I didn't steal nothin'!" he bellowed, glaring first at the sheriff and then at the sleuths.

"And you didn't threaten Rick into taking us into the swamp?" Joe asked sharply.

Clem grabbed the cell bars. "Of course not. It

was King George who did it! He set the whole thing up!"

"You're telling us that King George the Third of England is the one who burglarized that gallery in Bayport?" Frank asked, now seriously doubting the man's sanity.

"I'm telling you that King George is still taxing the colonies!" Clem continued to shout. "He took all that stuff instead of taxes."

The sheriff shook his head at his rantings and motioned for the boys to follow him back to his office. "That's about all I've been able to get out of Clem myself," he explained, closing the door behind him. "But the evidence is clear. I found these items in his garage this morning."

On a table in the corner of the office were a set of silverware and three canvases.

"Chet called me last night when you two didn't come back," the sheriff went on as he sat down and unwrapped a candy bar. "So I headed into the swamp with a couple of deputies to see if I could find you. Well, I didn't find *you*, but I did stumble on this stash of valuables when I went to Clem's house and searched his garage."

"Are these the things that were stolen from Durby McPhee?" Joe queried.

"At first I thought it was Clem's," the man replied. "But then I realized that these items were much more valuable than the stuff he handles. I remembered your story about the break-in in Bayport, so I called the Bayport police and checked with them. Sure enough, those are the objects stolen from McPhee's Antiques. That's why I had Clem arrested."

The sheriff, satisfied with his good work, grinned as he popped the last of the candy bar into his mouth. "By the way, what happened to you last night?"

Frank and Joe told him how they had been left in the swamp by the airboat operator and had to find their way back to town with the help of the middle-aged couple.

"You're lucky you were found." The sheriff smiled. "Or you might've had to spend another night out there."

"What do you make of Clem's story about the King?" Frank said, changing the subject.

The sheriff's face became thoughtful. "Clem seems to think the American Revolution is still in progress. His real name is Clemson Marion, the great-great-grandson of a man called Francis Marion, better known as the Swamp Fox. During the Revolution . . ."

"Clem told us all that," Joe interrupted. "What we don't know is why Clem believes King George is still alive and taxing the American colonies."

"I have my ideas about that too," the sheriff told the sleuths with a wink. "When we found the loot in his garage, we also found a red jacket and some other pieces of clothing that looked like part of an eighteenth-century English nobleman's costume. Now, I'm no psychologist, but it seems to me we have a case of a split personality here."

"Are you suggesting that Clem is playing the part of the Swamp Fox and King George at the same time?" Joe asked.

The sheriff nodded. "The old man is off his rocker. I think one day he dresses up in his tricornered hat to be the Swamp Fox. Next day, he dresses up as King George, the Swamp Fox's enemy, and parades around like that. It's a kind of crazy game he plays, acting out both the good guy and the bad guy. This way, he keeps the American Revolution still going in his head."

"Wow!" Chet spoke up. "If that's the case, he really is crazy. And you think the burglaries were done by the Swamp Fox-side of his personality?"

The sheriff nodded. "That's my guess. He burglarized the galleries because he believed they belonged to wealthy Tories, the supporters of the British during the Revolution. Then, as King George, he thought of the loot as being part of his taxes levied against the colonies."

"That's an interesting theory," Frank said in a doubtful tone.

"Well," the sheriff went on, "people around town have reported seeing the ghost of King George. He appeared late at night near the edge of the swamp. Five or six people swear they saw him just a couple of days ago."

"And you're sure it isn't just the swamp gas, combined with somebody's overactive imagination?" Joe asked, knowing that methane vapors rising from swampy waters often cause people to think they see a ghost.

"That's what I thought at first," the sheriff answered, swinging his feet up on his desk. "But then some pretty reliable fellows insist they saw the King's ghost as clear as day. That's when it came to me that Clem, who claims to be the mortal enemy of the King, may be dressing up as George the Third himself."

"But why would he pick so many different locations to steal the stuff from?" Frank reasoned. "Besides, this only represents a small part of what was stolen. Was this all you found?"

"Yep," the paunchy man replied. "The rest must be hidden in other places. I just hope Clem isn't too ornery to tell me what he did with it. Otherwise, I might be out there for months trying to find it all."

The boys asked to talk with Clem again, since at this point they were still not convinced that he was indeed the Bayport burglar, or that he suffered from a case of split personality.

"Clem, just tell me one thing," Frank said. "When and where did you first see the King?"

"Last year, at the Mardi Gras parade on Fat Tuesday," Clem replied. "And then I followed him to the party. Lots of people have parties on Fat Tuesday, you know."

"What party?"

"A party where he distributes the loot he has taken as taxes!" the old man cried.

"Where was the party?"

Clem shrugged. "In a beautiful house outside of town."

"Do you know how to get there?"

Clem shook his head. "I told you I followed the King. That's all I know."

"What about the silver and the paintings the sheriff found in your house?"

"He didn't find it in my house. He found it in my garage, which is always open whether I'm home or not. Someone put it there, and it weren't me! I didn't steal it, I tell ya, I didn't!"

The Hardys finally left the police station, unsure whether to believe the sheriff's theory or not.

"It makes sense to me," Chet stated. "Clem has already proven he's crazy. And they found the stolen stuff right where he lives."

"Well, he tells us this crazy story about King George and how he saw him at the Mardi Gras. Then he supposedly followed him to some party. It really sounds as if he made it all up."

"I know," Frank said as he climbed into the front seat of Rick's Chevy. "And yet, something bothers me about this whole thing. Have you ever seen this King, Rick?"

The boy nodded as he started his car. "I saw him a couple of nights ago when I was working on my boat's engine. Someone was creeping up behind the bushes a short way into the swamp. He had on a powdered wig and a red jacket, like the one the sheriff found. It was too dark and he was too far away for me to see his features, but he weren't no ghost."

"Who do you think it was?"

"That crazy old coot, Clem, of course. The man's as nutty as a fruitcake, and frankly, I'm scared of him."

Frank's brow was knitted in thought. "Is it possible to rent a plane at the local airport?" he asked Rick.

"I think so," the boy replied. "What for?"

"I want to follow a hunch. I know it sounds crazy, but maybe Clem's story isn't as far off base as we thought."

Joe snapped his fingers. "I see what you're getting at. If some guy other than Clem is masquerading as King George, he'd have his hideout in the swamp, maybe."

"Exactly," Frank agreed. "And the easiest way to spot it would be from the air."

Rick shrugged. "I think you're wasting your time, but I'll be glad to take you there."

Making a U turn, he headed away from town toward the small, private airfield. When they arrived, the Hardys made arrangements to rent a single-engine plane for the afternoon. Both were skilled pilots with valid licenses.

"Any word from Roger Mann?" Joe asked the airport manager, noticing the blue Cessna still parked near the hangar.

"Not yet," the manager replied. "I'll call you at the motel as soon as he shows up."

Minutes later, Frank and Joe were airborne in the rented plane. Since it was only a two-seater, it couldn't accommodate Chet and Rick, who drove back to town for a meal in the motel restaurant. Chet was happy to be left behind anyway, since he was hungry and wanted to see Sadie.

From above, the Okefenokee Swamp appeared as

an endless expanse of water and foliage. Joe piloted the plane, flying low over the ground and circling in a pattern that would cover the whole area in an hour or so.

Frank studied the terrain carefully, watching for any signs of hidden shacks or boats. "There's the spot where we were rescued," he said as they crossed the Suwannee River. "We sure were out in the middle of nowhere!"

Joe grinned. "Well, I'm glad we're up here now where the alligators can't get at us. Do you see any signs of life down below?"

"Nothing," his brother answered.

After thoroughly searching the swamp for more than two hours without a trace of success, the young detectives flew back toward the airport, disappointed.

"Scratch that idea," Joe said as the plane neared the runway. "I guess we'll—"

"Hey, watch out!" Frank shouted suddenly in alarm.

Taxiing out on the runway was the blue Cessna, blocking the boys' approach as they came in for their landing!

The voice of the controller crackled over the radio, ordering the Cessna to clear the runway. However, the pilot did not respond. Instead, he prepared to take off!

10 Razzle-Jazzle

"Hold on tight!" Joe shouted, throttling the engine and pulling up the stick. With one quick motion, he swung the small plane out of harm's way. The Cessna took off beneath them, turning westward once it was off the ground.

"That lunatic!" Frank cried out. "He could've killed us!"

"Let's follow him!" Joe said angrily.

"It wouldn't do any good. The Cessna's too fast."

"I guess you're right," Joe grumbled. He made a loop around the airport and brought the rental plane in for a landing. Once they were on the ground, the boys went straight to the manager's office.

"I didn't clear him for takeoff!" the manager, who doubled as the flight controller, said defensively.

"Did you tell him we wanted to talk to him?" Frank asked.

"That's what set him off!" the manager exclaimed. "The guy seemed determined to get out of here before you landed, with or without clearance."

Frank whistled. "That figures. Did you get a good look at the pilot and his passenger this time?"

"Roger Mann was still wearing his aviation glasses. All I can tell you is that he's about mid-sized, fairly thin, and has dark, curly hair. His passenger, as usual, kept himself out of sight. I only spotted him from a distance when he boarded the plane. He seemed to be tallish."

"What's the Cessna's destination?" Frank queried.

"His flight plan says Charlotte, North Carolina. But I think he lied. He took off in the opposite direction." The manager paused a moment, then added, "I overheard Mann say 'New Orleans' to his passenger before he got into the plane. Maybe that's where they're headed."

Frank and Joe thanked the man and walked outside. Soon Rick and Chet arrived to pick them up.

"See anything from up there?" Chet asked his buddies.

"No. But I think we found out something more important," Frank said, then explained how the blue, twin-engine Cessna had nearly caused an accident in the air in its attempt to avoid their questions.

"Clem couldn't have been the passenger on that plane," Chet declared. "He's in jail."

Frank was thoughtful as they drove away from the airport. "I wondered all along why we found so much evidence pointing to Clem as the burglar, and yet he seems an unlikely candidate," he said, looking out the window at the passing scenery. "Now I'm beginning to think that someone's trying to frame him."

"You mean somebody set this whole thing up to send us on a wild-goose chase after Clem?" Chet asked.

"Possibly," Frank replied. "Someone could've been using the rattlesnake emblem to lead us to Clem. Even the note we got to meet Clem in the swamp was probably faked."

"And the guy who did it might well be Roger Mann or his passenger," Joe added.

The airboat operator dropped the boys off at the Swamp Creek Inn, where they contacted Sam Radley in Bayport to see if he had uncovered a lead on Roger Mann. But all he could tell them was that the blue Cessna belonged to the pilot.

Frank and Joe then called their father, who offered to pay for their trip to New Orleans so they could track down Mann and the blue Cessna. "Just check with the airport before you go to make sure he really went there," Mr. Hardy added.

"Right. And if he did, we'll be able to visit Peter's grandfather and perhaps help him with this voodoo mumbo-jumbo," Frank said.

It turned out that the blue Cessna did, indeed, land in New Orleans. The boys packed their bags and checked out of the motel. They said good-bye to Sadie, and Chet wrote down her address, promising to send her a letter as soon as the mystery had been solved.

"And promise you won't tangle with any more rattlesnakes." The pretty girl laughed, waving.

It was late at night by the time the three youths arrived at the New Orleans airport. They were exhausted after the long bus trip to Savannah and the flight from there to New Orleans.

The streets of the old southern port were filled with thousands of people who had come for the yearly Mardi Gras festival. Many wore brightly colored costumes, and all were in the spirit of the springtime celebration, swarming through the streets and moving to the lively music of dixieland jazz that poured out from the open doors of crowded restaurants.

"I'm tired," Chet complained. "Let's check into a hotel and do our investigating tomorrow."

"We don't need a hotel," Joe told him as he led them down Bourbon Street, probably the most famous street in the history of American jazz music. "Peter Walker said his grandfather would let us stay at his club. He has a couple of bedrooms upstairs."

Pushing through the crowd, the boys arrived at a club with the word STRETCH'S written in big red lettering above the front door. A dixieland band was in full swing inside, but there weren't too many customers.

"That must be Stretch up there on stage," Joe commented, looking at a big trombone player in the band. "He's supposed to be one of the top guys around."

Stretch Walker was indeed one of the best dixieland musicians still alive. New Orleans had been the birthplace of jazz, and just a handful of musicians were still living who could boast of having helped invent the country's only original musical form. Stretch was one of them.

The sleuths took seats and listened as the band played "When the Saints Go Marching In" with Stretch taking the solo. Once the set was over,

Frank and Joe went to the stage and introduced themselves.

Stretch smiled from ear to ear when he learned that they were his grandson's friends. "Peter called and told me you boys might be coming down for a vacation," he said. "So I got your rooms all ready for you." He led them to a nearby table, and the Hardys sat down with him.

"Actually, we didn't come here on vacation," Frank told the old jazz trombonist. "We're working on a case. And Peter is worried that you might be in some kind of trouble, possibly involving voodoo. We promised him we'd check into it."

Stretch's smile left his face as Frank explained about the dead bird with Stretch's name written nine times on a piece of paper folded up in its mouth. "The bird was sent from New Orleans," Frank said in conclusion.

Stretch shook his head in anger. "Those bums!" he nearly shouted. "Now they're after my family!" He cursed under his breath, then looked up at the young visitors. "I didn't want my family to know." He groaned. "But now I guess I have no choice."

"So you *are* in some kind of trouble?" Frank asked.

Holding his head in his hands, Stretch Walker sighed. "I don't know how to explain it, but there's some kind of voodoo cult that's out to get me—"

The trombonist was interrupted by a commotion in the club. Several heavily costumed men had entered and were roughly shoving their way toward the stage.

"That's them!" Stretch yelled, rising to his feet.

The men were masked and their bodies were striped with colored paint. Some of them had even plumed themselves with bright feathers that flowed from their heads and arms.

Before the boys had time to react, the men jumped up on the stage, where they began to dance wildly, kicking over the players' instruments and hooting like wild men. One of them lit a stink bomb, which he swung from a string over his head, producing a thick cloud of smelly smoke. At the same time, he ordered everyone to leave before he burned the club down!

With Stretch in the lead, the Hardys hurled themselves at the costumed men. Blows were exchanged, but the thugs far outnumbered Stretch and the boys. They drove the Hardys from the stage before running out themselves past the stunned onlookers.

"I'm going after them!" Joe cried, picking himself up from the floor. He slid through the crowd and chased the escaping intruders into the street. A minute later he returned, badly beaten. His nose was bloody and the side of his face was already puffing up from a heavy blow, but he was smiling.

"I ripped one of the guys' masks off and got a good look at his mug!" Joe said as he sat down and wiped the blood from his nose. "I also landed a couple of nice punches myself."

Frank looked grimly at his brother. "Here," he said, wrapping a napkin around some ice from an empty glass on a table. "Put this on your nose. It'll help stop the bleeding."

Joe took the homemade ice pack, and Frank turned to Stretch, who was watching with dismay as the frightened patrons hurried out the door.

"What was that all about?" the older Hardy questioned.

Stretch shrugged. "I was about to tell you. Those guys are members of a voodoo cult. They've been harassing me for weeks, both with shows like the one you just saw and with threats of hexes they're putting on me. Several of my employees have already quit, and right now my band is in danger of breaking up. That would put me out of business."

"Have you talked to the police?" Joe queried.

"Yes, but they haven't done much about it. They don't take this voodoo as anything more than a joke. And now with Mardi Gras on, they're too busy dealing with the crowds to pay any attention to this kind of thing."

105

"Do *you* take it seriously?" Frank asked the old jazz trombonist.

"I don't know," Stretch said nervously. "But with my people quitting work and the way my business has suffered, I'd better start taking it seriously."

"And you don't know why they're after you?" Frank went on.

"Only that they told me in the beginning that this club was the home of some voodoo god, and that they wanted me out so the god could come back or something. First I thought they were a bunch of harmless crazies."

"Well, voodoo god or not, those men are not harmless," Joe said, applying the ice pack to his swollen cheek.

Stretch nodded. "That's why I didn't dare leave here to go to Bayport for Peter's game. I was afraid these guys would tear the place apart in my absence." A disturbing thought then crossed the jazz player's mind. "How do you think the voodoo cult got my grandson's address? And why would they send him that dead bird?"

"We thought it was a prank," Frank admitted. "Now I'm not sure."

Stretch sighed loudly. "I don't have any enemies. I never did anything to those people. Why would they want to harass me?"

106

"That's what we plan to find out," Joe assured the old man. "Frank and I are what you might call amateur detectives. Chet here is—hey, where's Chet?"

11 The Witch's Hint

Both boys had forgotten about their chubby friend, and suddenly realized he wasn't with them. Anxiously, they scanned the club's interior.

"Chet!" Joe cried, spotting a motionless body in the corner near the stage.

Afraid their friend had been seriously injured during the fight with the voodoo gang, the Hardys ran up to him. Chet's eyes were closed and he lay slumped against the wall.

Joe bent over the inert figure. "Chet, Chet, are you okay?" he cried, shaking his friend into consciousness.

Chet slowly opened his eyes. "What—what's the matter?" he stammered groggily.

"Are you all right?" Joe asked.

"I think I am," Chet replied. "At least I was until that chair conked me on the head. I guess I kind of passed out." Suddenly, Chet noticed Joe's bruises. "Oh boy, what happened to your face?"

Frank shook his head grimly. "We'll tell you on the way upstairs. Let's go get some sleep."

Stretch Walker showed the young detectives to their second-floor bedrooms, where Chet, Frank, and Joe stayed awake to watch the crowd of people who still filled the street below their windows.

In the morning, the boys called the private airport that the blue Cessna had flown to. But again, the manager had no record of where the pilot was staying or who his passenger was.

Frank grunted. "We're no better off than we were at Swamp Creek. Roger Mann could be anywhere. And with the city full of strangers, it'll be next to impossible to track him down!"

Joe nodded. "Yet we'll have to find him. If he's connected with the burglaries, he could be in New Orleans to dispose of the stolen property."

"Not only that, we'll have to catch him in the act, otherwise we have no case on him," Frank pointed out.

"So what do we do?" Chet asked in frustration.

"Go to the police and see if we can get a list of hotels in the area," Frank replied. "It's a slim chance, but something might come of it."

At headquarters, they told Chief Lloyd about the case they were working on and gave him the property list their father had written up. He promised to call them at the club if any items on the list turned up.

"As for Roger Mann, let me put our switchboard on to help you," the chief offered. "I'll have them call all the hotels and guest houses in town. If you went to every one of them, you'd still be here for next year's Mardi Gras."

The boys thanked him and left. As they walked down the street, Joe suddenly stopped and pointed to a small shop with dirty windows and a sign that read WITCHCRAFT, MAGIC, VOODOO.

"Let's go in here," he said.

"What do you have in mind?" Chet inquired after they had entered the little place.

"Maybe the proprietor knows something about that voodoo cult," Frank replied.

The shopkeeper, a young woman, sat in a thickly upholstered armchair in the far corner of the room. She wore a long, flowing gown and several bead necklaces. Her arms were ringed with silver bracelets, some of which were crafted in ornate patterns.

The walls of the shop were lined with jars of herbs and different colored liquids, giving the impression of an ancient drugstore.

"May I help you with something?" the woman asked, getting up from her chair.

"We were hoping you'd know where to locate a certain voodoo cult," Frank told her, then described the men who had invaded Stretch's club the night before.

"Could have been anybody." The shopkeeper shrugged. "During Mardi Gras, lots of people put on all kinds of acts. These men probably were a bunch of pranksters, pretending to be voodoo worshippers. Real voodoo cults keep pretty much to themselves. They don't want attention."

"These guys were more than pranksters," Joe said and pulled from his pocket the remains of the stink bomb that he had found on the club's stage that morning. "They were burning this stuff at Stretch's. Maybe you can tell us what it's made of?"

The woman took the fragments and placed them on the counter. Then she broke them apart further and began smelling separate pieces, identifying the substances that had gone into the bomb.

Once finished, she appeared lost in thought for a moment. "All these things can be bought here," she said finally. "In fact, someone was in my shop the other day and purchased just these items. I don't know if he was a member of that voodoo group, though."

111

"Do you have a record of the sale?" Frank asked, growing excited.

"He paid by check," the young woman said. "I haven't cashed it yet. It should have his name and address on it."

She went through her cash register to find the man's check, then wrote something on a piece of paper.

"Here's the address," she said. "The fellow's name is Maurice Duboise."

"Thanks," Frank said, taking the piece of paper and slipping it into his shirt pocket. "By the way, do you practice voodoo yourself? We'd like to know more about it."

"No." The woman smiled. "I'm a witch."

The boys' eyes went wide and they stood silent, not sure how to react.

"But," she continued, enjoying their surprise, "I know someone who's an authority on voodoo. He'd be happy to tell you all you want to know." She wrote another name and address on a piece of paper. "His name's Paul Valent. Just say I sent you."

The boys thanked her and left the strange little shop. First they headed for the address of Mr. M. Duboise, which turned out to be a two-family house in the French Quarter, one of the oldest sections of New Orleans. No answer came when they rang the buzzer marked with his name.

"His apartment is on the top floor," Frank said to Chet. "I want you to wait across the street and watch his window. If you see anybody enter or leave, call us. Meantime, Joe and I will be visiting that voodoo authority the shopkeeper told us about."

Chet wasn't pleased to be left behind to stake out the apartment, but he agreed to do his part. After taking down Valent's phone number, he settled himself in a doorway across the street.

Paul Valent, the voodoo expert, also lived in the French Quarter. He was a portly old college professor who had studied voodoo and the black arts as a hobby since he had retired. He showed Frank and Joe around his apartment, which was filled with collected masks and other knickknacks used in various superstitious rites, including voodoo. He loved having company, and bent the boys' ears with stories of the history of voodoo: how it had originated in Africa as a worship of snakes and then had spread to Haiti and the southern United States.

"Yes, it's still practiced in this area," the portly man told them. "Even recently, people have seen headless chickens, cats, goats, and other animals floating in the Mississippi River, which were probably the result of voodoo ceremonies."

"What about the gang at Stretch's club?" Joe

queried. "Do they sound like real voodoo worshippers to you?"

The professor looked puzzled. "Not really. That story about Stretch Walker's place being the home of a voodoo god doesn't sound typical of the superstition. Of course, a lot of voodoo today is practiced by small groups, who have changed the original concept to suit their own ideas. So anything is possible."

"What we're trying to figure out," Frank said, "is whether this so-called cult consists of a bunch of superstitious weirdos or whether they're using voodoo to cover up some sort of illegal scheme."

"I couldn't say," the professor said, raising his eyebrows. "At Mardi Gras time, people do all kinds of crazy stunts. The whole city goes bananas."

Just then, the phone rang. Valent picked it up, then handed it to Frank. "It's for you," he said.

"Someone went to the apartment." Chet's voice came anxiously over the receiver. "A man. He was driving a green Cadillac. I saw him get out, and then again in the window of Duboise's place. He stayed for a few minutes, then took off."

"Did you talk to him?" Frank asked.

"Are you kidding? He was a big, mean-looking guy. I wanted to get you over here, but he left before I could find a phone."

114

"Okay," Frank said. "Go back to Stretch's place. We'll be there in a few minutes."

After thanking the retired professor for his help, Frank and Joe returned to the club and met Chet at the front door. "Somebody slapped some paint on Stretch's door," the chubby boy reported. "See? It's a mess."

The young detectives noted red markings.

"I suppose with all these people in the streets, nothing is safe from vandals," Joe said sadly.

They let themselves in with a key the jazz trombonist had given them, and found the interior deserted.

"That's funny," Joe said. "Stretch said he'd be here this afternoon."

Frank started for the stairway leading to the second floor. "He'll probably show up in a little— hey, here's a note!"

He picked up a piece of paper from the bottom step and read it out loud:

BOYS: MESSAGE FROM HEAD-
QUARTERS. THEY CAN'T LO-
CATE R.M. MEET ME AT THE
GUMBO DINER, NINE MILES
WEST ON LEVY ROAD, AS
SOON AS POSSIBLE. STRETCH.

12 Voodoo!

"Do you suppose the note is really from Stretch?"
Chet asked anxiously.

"I don't believe the sergeant would have given
the message to anyone but him," Frank said. "But—
you never know. We'll find out for sure when we get
there."

The three boys ran out into the street and hailed a
taxi. When they gave the driver the address, he
turned in his seat and eyed them with a frown.

"Are you sure that's where you want me to take
you? Do you know what's going on out there?"

"No. What?" Frank asked.

"Voodoo, that's what," the cab driver told them.
"I wouldn't go near the place myself. They'd as soon
put a hex on you as look at you!"

"Take us there," Frank said firmly to the superstitious man. "You can drop us off down the road if you want."

The driver shrugged and headed for Levy Road, which ran northwest from the city. The sun was well down by the time he pulled over to the curb to let them out. After receiving his fare, he instructed them to follow the road another hundred yards on foot to the Gumbo Diner on the left.

"Will you wait for us here?" Chet asked, uneasy about being left in this strange place.

"No way," the cabbie replied. "I'm getting out of here, pronto!" With that, he drove off in a cloud of dust.

"How are we going to get back?" Chet wondered.

"We'll find a way," Frank said. "If Stretch is here, he'll have his car, anyway."

The diner was a small, dingy-looking place, and the trio approached it cautiously.

"Hey, boys!" a voice suddenly called in a hushed tone from behind some bushes.

Frank and Joe swung around to see Stretch Walker stepping out of the underbrush.

"Stretch! What are—" Chet began, but the old man motioned for him to stop talking and follow him instead into the bushes.

"You missed the first part," Stretch said in a whisper as he led the way into the woods.

"What are you talking about?" Frank inquired.

"See for yourselves," Stretch replied and pointed to a clearing up ahead, where a voodoo ceremony was in progress. An elaborately costumed man presided over it, sitting in an elevated chair. At its foot stood a long cage containing a snake. A woman sat next to him, also adorned in brightly colored pieces of cloth and jewelry. A large fire burned in the center of the clearing, illuminating thirty or more people gathered on the ground in a wide circle.

"I think they're about to initiate a new member," Stretch whispered, crouching behind a log just outside the clearing.

Frank, Joe, and Chet watched as the head voodoo man picked a stick out of the fire and drew a ring in the dirt in front of him. Another man rose from among the worshippers and stepped into the ring.

"That's the one they're initiating," Stretch explained. "The man and woman in the strange costumes are the king and queen. They're in charge of the ceremony."

Frank and Joe exchanged glances, both struck at the second mention of kings in recent days. They watched as the voodoo king tapped the new member on the head with his stick, then began an African-sounding chant:

EH! EH! BOMBA, HEN, HEN!
CANGA BAFIO TE,
CANGA MOUNE DE LE!

As the chant continued, the new cult member squirmed and danced around the ring, writhing in a snakelike motion. He then was handed a cup of liquid, and once he had consumed it, he began to dance even more furiously, going into convulsions in the center of the ring.

At last, the man stopped his wild dance. He was led to a makeshift altar, where he took an oath to obey the laws of the cult and worship the serpent.

After the initiation ceremony, the king placed his foot on the cage containing the snake. A shock seemed to go through his body, which was transmitted to the voodoo queen, then through the whole cult. They all started shaking wildly, writhing and thrashing about on the ground. Once they had exhausted themselves, the ceremony was over.

"Boy, that was quite a show!" Chet said, gawking at the cultists.

"What brought you here?" Frank asked, turning to Stretch.

The jazz trombonist stood up. "One of these guys was painting some strange markings on my door when I arrived at the club this afternoon," he said, frowning.

"Oh, is that what it was?" Chet asked. "We saw it and figured vandals did it."

"No," Stretch went on. "It was the voodoo gang. So I hid around the corner until the guy finished, and followed him out here in my car. Then I went back to find you boys, but you weren't there. I left the note and returned."

"Well, we found out one thing," Joe said. "These guys are really into voodoo. They're not just pretending to be to cover up something else."

"But what do they want from Stretch?" Chet asked. "Why are they picking on him?"

"I wish I knew," Frank said. "Let's go back to the diner. Maybe we can eavesdrop and learn something."

The group circled through the woods. In the rear of the little eating place, they found a parking lot with several cars in it. Obviously, they belonged to the cultists.

"Those people are going to have to change their clothes before going home," Joe said.

Frank nodded. "Let's see if we can spy on them. Stretch, why don't you get your car in case we have to leave in a hurry, okay?"

"Sure thing," the old man said with a grin and left.

The boys moved closer to the parking lot.

"Hey!" Chet cried out softly. "There's the green

121

Cadillac I saw at the apartment this afternoon. It belongs to Maurice Duboise!"

"That figures," Frank said. "Let's move up to the side of the place and see what we can see through the windows."

The boys cautiously approached the diner. They peered inside, but all they could glimpse were empty booths. There were no customers, and there was no sign of the voodoo gang.

"They must be in another room," Frank whispered. "Maybe—"

He heard a rustle behind them and turned around. Six men were converging on them from both sides!

"Run!" Frank cried out and bolted away from the diner. But one of the men was close enough to cut him off and trip him. Frank sprawled headlong on the asphalt!

He got to his feet in a split second and kicked his attacker. A brawl ensued, with the young detectives outnumbered two to one by the voodoo thugs!

"Let's get out of here!" Chet bellowed.

Luckily, Stretch had gotten his car and was now driving up to the scene. While the gang scattered to get out of his way, the boys managed to jump in. One of the cultists tried to drag Joe from the front seat, but Joe kicked furiously and got rid of him. Two others hung on to the fenders. Stretch stepped on the gas, then made a series of sharp turns that threw the gang members off.

"Wow!" Joe cried. "That was too close for comfort!"

"They must have seen us walking toward the diner," Frank said glumly.

Joe nodded. "And wouldn't you know, my friend I hassled with before was among them again. I'm glad I had a chance to kick him in the shin."

"I'm glad, too," Frank grumbled. "Because I got it in the jaw today, but good!" He gingerly felt the swelling on the side of his face.

"The guy who first tripped you was Duboise," Chet told Frank.

"He's also the voodoo king," Frank replied. "I can tell even though he wore a costume."

Stretch Walker spoke up at last. "I know Maurice Duboise," he said. "He's an old dixieland musician. Used to play bass back when Satchmo was gigging around town."

"Did you ever play with Satchmo?" Chet broke in, referring to the legendary Louis Armstrong, who had been nicknamed Satchmo in his early years.

The trombonist nodded. "Once or twice. We did some mean jammin'."

"So you know the voodoo king personally," Frank said, coming back to the matter at hand.

"Yes. But I haven't seen him in years," Stretch

said. "He was sent to prison some time ago. All I heard was that he got out and ended up as part owner of another club in town."

"Does he have a personal grudge against you?" Joe queried.

The trombone player shrugged. "No. But he was always kind of a wild guy. When he started getting mixed up with a bad crowd, the other musicians wouldn't have anything more to do with him."

"You said he's now part owner of a club?" Frank asked.

"That's right. It's called Jazz Alley. Actually, it's a little way outside town. Small place."

"And you have no idea why he and his gang are giving you trouble?"

Stretch shook his head. "None."

Frank sat a moment in thought while looking out the window. They were reentering the city and traffic was already beginning to grow thick, slowing their pace to a crawl.

"Has anyone offered to buy your club recently?" Frank finally asked on a hunch.

Stretch knitted his brows. "Yes. In fact, someone wanted to buy it just a few weeks ago. But the offer was too low, and I don't want to sell anyway."

"Who made the offer?" the young detective continued.

"A fellow by the name of Sedgwick Stokes,"

Stretch replied. "He's in the real-estate business. Banner Realty's the name of his company. His office is just a couple of blocks from my place."

A few minutes later, they were all back at the club. The street still swarmed with revelers, but only a few customers were inside.

"It should be jammed by now," Stretch said with a groan. "Those voodoo maniacs are driving me out of business!"

"I think that's exactly what they have in mind," Frank said.

"But why?" the old jazzman wondered.

"Let's call the police and have them put those crooks under arrest!" Chet suggested.

"We wouldn't be able to pin much on them," Frank said, shaking his head. "There's something behind this charade of voodoo, and we'll have to find out what it is."

Joe nodded. "And bringing in the police might blow our chances of doing that."

"Just don't take too long," Stretch pleaded. "With business like it's been, I might be forced to sell the club, even if it's to Stokes."

"Don't be too hasty," Frank warned. "We have a few rocks to turn over before we get to the bottom of this, and Sedgwick Stokes will be the first one."

"I think we'll find worms underneath," Joe added.

"What about that red stuff the voodoo clown put on my door earlier?" the trombonist asked. "What do you suppose that's all about?"

The Hardys and Chet checked out the front door still covered with the red markings put on in the afternoon. There was no particular design, just paint slapped on with a brush. The boys puzzled over it for a few minutes before Frank knelt down and scraped some off with his nail.

"Hey!" he exclaimed. "This isn't paint. It's blood!"

13 Nothing But Trouble

"Most likely it's chicken blood," Joe figured. "Nonetheless, it's pretty spooky."

"I'll say!" Chet agreed.

The boys went inside to tell Stretch about the blood, but the trombonist was on stage, playing with his band to the small audience.

"Let's go out to dinner and then get to bed early," Frank suggested. "We have a lot of work to do in the morning and I want to get an early start."

When they came back from a nearby restaurant, Chet stayed up to listen to the music for a while, but Frank and Joe retired to their room. In the morning, they left their still sleeping friend and walked to Banner Realty.

Sedgwick Stokes was in a back office of the large

building. He was a small man, who wore dark glasses. The light tan suit he had on was a little too large for his frame, and it looked as if it hadn't been pressed for some time.

"What can I do for you?" he asked the boys, giving them a businesslike grin.

"We're friends of Stretch Walker's," Frank said as he stepped up to the desk. "We hear you recently made an offer to buy his club. He told us that the offer was very low. What made you think he'd sell at that price?"

"Well—" The broker seemed to fumble over his reply. "I heard that Stretch had come into some hard times lately. So I figured he might be interested in selling the club and I made him an offer."

"Then you know about the voodoo gang that has been harassing him?" Joe took over the questioning.

The little man grew wary. "Yes, in fact, I do. What are you driving at?"

Joe leaned slightly over the desk and looked Stokes straight in the eye. "We just wondered whether you and that voodoo cult had joined forces to make Stretch sell out at a cheap price!" he said evenly.

Stokes laughed nervously and shifted in his chair. "That's ridiculous. I'm just a businessman who saw the opportunity of picking up a piece of property at a good price, that's all. I have no idea who those crazy voodoo guys are, or why they're giving your friend trouble. Now, if you'll excuse me, I have a lot of work to do."

Convinced that Stokes was indeed trying to cover up something, Frank and Joe left the office.

"It may not be easy to prove," Joe said when they were outside. "But I bet that guy has something to do with Stretch's problem."

"I agree," Frank said. "Let's check into Stokes's business dealings some more. Perhaps Dad can find out something for us."

Joe nodded. "We haven't talked to him in a couple of days anyway. Maybe he knows more about the burglaries."

"And Sam may have uncovered a clue to that Cessna's pilot," Frank added. "Like where he's staying or who his passenger is."

On their way to the jazz club, the boys saw that the city was even more crowded with Mardi Gras activity than the day before. People dressed in bizarre outfits paraded up and down the streets, filling the downtown area with festivity.

"This place is really alive," Joe remarked as he looked around.

"That's because tomorrow is the last day of Mardi Gras," Frank said. "They call it Fat Tuesday, the wildest part of the festival. There'll be parades going on all day and into the night."

Joe glanced behind him as he took in the colorful scene, then quickly grabbed Frank's arm. "I think someone's following us," he said anxiously. "Take a look."

Pretending to gaze idly about, the dark-haired boy glanced over his shoulder. He noticed a costumed man duck out of the way about twenty feet behind them. He was dressed up in the same kind of outfit the voodoo gang had worn in Stretch's club!

"You're right," Frank said, turning around. "Now those thugs are after *us*!"

Hoping to lose the man in the crowd, the Hardys quickened their pace. They glanced behind them again at the end of the block and noticed to their chagrin that the man they had spotted was walking faster now. In addition, several other voodoo worshippers were hurrying along with him, trying to catch up with the boys!

"Quick! Down this street!" Frank hissed, making a sharp right.

The young detectives turned the corner and broke into a run down a main avenue. The men behind them started to run, too, pushing revelers roughly out of their way.

The avenue was not only thronged with tourists, but an organized parade was underway. Brass bands marched down the street in file, and a few floats glided along between them. Yet the men made good progress.

"They're gaining on us!" Joe shouted, looking back.

"Follow me," Frank said, dodging through the crowd. "I have an idea."

With the dark-haired boy in the lead, the Hardys dashed into the parade itself. They ducked under the skirts of a float and disappeared from sight. Except for the platform truck on which it was mounted, the float was mostly hollow underneath, and the boys kept pace with it for a few city blocks before creeping out again.

Joe scanned the avenue carefully. "We've lost them," he finally said with a sigh of relief.

"For the time being we have," Frank agreed. "Let's get back to Stretch's."

When they arrived at the club, they found Chet just getting out of bed.

"Did I miss anything?" he asked his companions.

Frank grinned. "Yes, and it's just as well you did. I'm not sure you could've kept up the pace."

"Kept up the pace?" Chet yawned. "What pace?"

"Never mind," Joe chuckled. "Just remember to be on the lookout for that voodoo gang. They're on to *us* now."

Chet looked unhappy, but Joe did not explain any

further. Instead, he went out into the hall and, using a wall phone, dialed their home in Bayport.

"It's about time you called." Aunt Gertrude's voice came loud and clear over the receiver. "Your father's been wanting to talk to you."

The phone went silent for a moment, then Mr. Hardy picked it up. "I've been in touch with the police in Georgia," he informed his son. "Rattlesnake Clem has been set free on bail."

"That's good," Joe said, and explained that they felt Clem was innocent. "We think he was set up, but we haven't had any luck locating Roger Mann. He and his passenger might be behind this whole thing."

"Sam checked Mann's record," Mr. Hardy said, "but couldn't find anything of interest. The man just hires out his services as a pilot."

"Do you know who's paying him now?"

"That's the mystery," his father replied. "The other pilots Mann associates with usually know whom he's taking out. But he's been very close-mouthed about his recent client, as if he were covering up something."

"It figures." Joe sighed. Then he told his father about Stretch Walker's problems with the voodoo cult.

"I want you to be careful," Mr. Hardy warned. "That group sounds like bad news. But I'll call Peter

Walker and let him know you're working on it."

"Thanks, Dad," Joe said.

"One last thing," Mr. Hardy said before hanging up. "The Georgia police told me that Clem asked permission to go to New Orleans for a week. Said he needed to pick up some merchandise for his business."

"H'm. That's interesting," Joe said. "I wonder if we'll run into him."

After he finished talking with his father, he told Frank the news. "Clem's coming here," he said with a look of curiosity on his face. "They let him out on bail."

"Coming here?" Frank asked. "What for?"

"Supposedly to buy some stuff for his business."

Chet, who had been in the bathroom washing up, now walked over to the boys.

"Has Stretch been around today?" Frank asked him.

"I guess so," Chet replied. "I heard a bunch of men downstairs earlier. They were making a real racket. I figured it was Stretch and the members of his band arguing about something."

"And you didn't go see what it was?" Joe questioned in disbelief.

Chet threw up his hands. "No. Why should I? I wanted to sleep."

A chill ran down Frank's spine as he realized that

Stretch might have been the victim of the same men who had tried to catch the Hardys earlier!

"I hope we haven't made things worse than they already were." He groaned.

"So do I," Joe said. "Duboise wasn't too happy about our visit to his voodoo ceremony yesterday. Maybe he decided to play rough."

"Are you saying that they may have kidnapped Stretch?" Chet moaned, suddenly feeling guilty about having slept through the whole thing.

"I don't know. Let's just sit tight for a while," Frank advised. "If Stretch isn't here by this evening, we'll call the police!"

14 The Cryptic Song

Leaving the club, the three boys visited the city government building to check through records of local properties. The files showed that Sedgwick Stokes had already bought several jazz clubs in New Orleans. Further investigation revealed that he had closed them all and changed them into other businesses. The only exception was Jazz Alley, the club in which both Stokes and Duboise were partners.

"I think I know what Stokes is up to," Joe muttered as they left the building. "He and Duboise work together into scaring owners of other jazz clubs to sell out to cut the competition."

Frank nodded. "No wonder he knew about the voodoo cult. He's probably part of it!"

"So Jazz Alley ought to be our next stop," Chet deduced.

Frank looked at his watch. "First, let's go back to Stretch's and see if he's there."

Carefully keeping an eye out for the voodoo gang, the young people made their way toward the club. Arriving at the door, they were just about to go in, when from behind a pile of crates stacked in the alley next to the building a ghostly figure appeared!

It was draped in a white sheet, with only two small holes cut out for the eyes! Chet cringed in the doorway when he saw the "ghost" taking a step in his direction. At the same time, Frank and Joe put up their fists, prepared to fight.

"Boys, boys," came a voice from behind the sheet. "It's me, Stretch!"

The young detectives relaxed their guard.

"Wha—" Joe began.

"Shh! This way." The trombonist cut him off in a hushed tone and motioned for them to follow him.

Bursting with curiosity over Stretch's costume, the boys went with him down the alley and into a crowded fruit market. There the old jazzman pulled the sheet away from his face.

"Hi!" He grinned. "I hope I didn't scare you."

"What's all this about?" Joe asked, bewildered.

"Duboise and his gang paid me a visit early this

136

morning while you were out," Stretch told them. "They said they wanted to talk to you, but I was afraid they were planning to rough you up. They were about to look for you upstairs, when another guy came in and said he'd spotted you in the street. Then they left."

"But why the disguise?" Joe queried.

"Duboise came back this afternoon and the whole gang is in the club waiting for you right now," Stretch replied. "I sneaked out so I could catch you before you went in. The sheet is so they wouldn't recognize me out here."

"Thanks," Frank said, and breathed a sigh of relief.

The trombone player grinned. "It's the least I could do after the trouble I've made for you."

"Well, what'll we do now?" Chet asked.

"Seems like the perfect time to visit Jazz Alley," Joe suggested. "We'll check out their club while they're waiting for us in Stretch's."

Finding pieces of fruit cartons lying around the market, the boys made bizarre costumes for themselves, and when all were well disguised, they entered the street and walked to Stretch's car, which was parked four blocks away. From there, they drove to the outskirts of town.

Jazz Alley was a low wooden-frame building on

the far side of a shopping mall. It was dark by the time they got there, but too early for the music to start.

"Do we go in with those boxes on our heads?" Chet asked.

Stretch shook his head. "That's too obvious. Besides, we won't need our disguises. The place is dark, and we'll get a table in the corner somewhere. Let's leave the costumes in the car."

The group went into the club, picked a secluded table, and sat down to a big dinner of spicy creole-style food while they waited for the place to fill up.

"Tell us more about Duboise," Frank said once he had finished his first plateful of food.

"Well," Stretch said, "as I mentioned before, back in the old days he and I gigged together every now and then. He always wanted to be the center of attention, though. Always tried to run the show."

"What was he sent to prison for?" Frank asked.

"Don't rightly know, but I think it was theft. We other musicians kept our distance from him and his crowd by that time."

"Looks like he's doing pretty well now," Chet remarked, gesturing around him at the lavish club.

Stretch Walker frowned. "He wasn't doing so well before those other clubs in the city shut down. Now, with all that competition gone, more people are coming out here."

"Does Duboise play in the band?" Joe questioned.

"Plays in the band, leads the band, and owns a good percentage of the club." Stretch grunted. "He's finally getting to be what he always wanted to be, top dog."

Frank finished his soda, trying to rinse out the burning feeling left in his mouth by the spicy food. "I bet Duboise and Stokes have a deal going," he said. "Stokes buys up the clubs around town to cut competition, and Duboise sees to it that the owners are scared enough to sell."

"Let's hope—" Joe started, then his attention was drawn to the front door. "There he is now," the boy said.

Covering their faces with their hands, the group stopped talking as Maurice Duboise entered the club and walked through a door behind the stage. At the same time, the place began filling with people. Soon it was jammed. Then the house lights went down and the stage was illuminated as Duboise's band came on. Duboise himself got the spotlight, introducing the musicians and leading them into their first number.

Stretch ordered another round of soft drinks as they listened from the back corner of the room. Frank and Joe kept an eye on the steady flow of customers coming through the front door.

"There's Stokes!" Joe said suddenly, noticing the real-estate investor walk in.

The man strutted toward the stage and took a reserved table near the front of the room. As he did, the band finished the number they were playing. A few minutes later, they started up again.

"That's a pretty song," Frank said, leaning toward Stretch. "What is it? I never heard it before."

Stretch Walker leaned back in his seat with pride. "*I* wrote that song about forty years ago. You don't hear it much up North, but it's played every now and again in these parts. It's about the place I was born, up in the Mississippi Delta."

"I like it!" Chet said, tapping his fingers and feet to the upbeat rhythm.

"I like it myself," the trombonist admitted. "Except for the fact that Maurice Duboise is singing it."

Duboise, wearing dark glasses and a dinner jacket, was at the microphone. His singing was more like shouting, which didn't seem to fit the wistful nature of the song.

Suddenly, Stretch's smile dropped from his face. "He's singing the wrong words!" he growled angrily. "I didn't write that! The bum's changing it all around!"

"Maybe he just doesn't remember the text," Frank said, trying to calm Stretch down.

"Of course he does! He played in the band with

me when I used to sing it," the musician objected. "We must've played it at least a hundred times."

When the song was over, the sleuths had to almost bodily prevent Stretch from yelling out and making their presence known. At the same point, Sedgwick Stokes stood up from his chair and walked out the door, as if he had only come in to hear that one song.

"Should we follow him?" Joe asked, getting ready to leave.

Frank appeared to be lost in thought and didn't respond to his brother's question. A moment later, he turned to address Stretch. "How were the words in the song changed?"

"Well," the trombonist began, not sure of what the youth was driving at. "Not all of them were different. Just a few lines."

"Which ones?" Frank asked.

"Let's see," Stretch said, trying to remember Duboise's mistakes. "One verse was supposed to be—" He began to sing in a low voice:

LORD, TAKE ME WHERE THE LIVING'S FREE
DOWN BY THE RIVER THAT RUNS TO THE SEA
WHERE THE WATER'S CLEAR AS THE DEEP BLUE SKY
AND I'LL BE GOING BY AND BY . . .

"But the way he sang it," Stretch went on, "was like this:

> LORD, TAKE ME WHERE THE LIVING'S
> FREE
> DOWN BY THE RIVER *at old Belle*
> *Lee*
> *Gold and silver will be waiting there*
> *In a sunlit room up a winding stair*

Frank snapped his fingers. "I bet the changed words were a message to Stokes."

"Message?" Chet wondered aloud.

"Right," Joe answered, picking up Frank's thought. "And it could be the key to this whole mystery!"

15 *Here Comes the King!*

"Wait a minute," Frank said after thinking it through. "Why would Duboise want to send such a message to Stokes? They're partners, they can talk together any time."

Joe nodded. "You have a point there."

"Maybe the message was to someone else, and Stokes came in to make sure the other party was there to receive it," Chet suggested.

Frank nodded. "That's possible."

The group paid for the dinner and drinks, then left Jazz Alley. They returned to Stretch's club, making sure before they entered that the voodoo gang wasn't still lying in wait for them.

"I'm not tired yet," Chet said. "Let's go back out and watch the parade."

"Good idea." Joe grinned. "It should be in full swing now."

Deciding they had done enough sleuthing for the day, the boys grabbed half masks from a basket that stood near the cash register and left the club to join in the Mardi Gras festival, which included a fireworks display that a local organization had advertised.

The streets were filled with tourists, some of them costumed and others not. A parade was in full swing, and many of the merrymakers danced to the music that filled the air. Scores of floats glided down the avenue, all brightly lit with an array of colored lights.

"This is some scene!" Chet laughed as they pushed through the crowd.

"I think the fireworks are this way." Joe pointed. "I saw them being set up this morning."

When the boys rounded a corner, they watched huge spinning wheels showering the sky with sparkles and Roman candles spraying fountains of light into the air.

"Wait a second. Do you guys hear that?" Frank said suddenly, looking toward the parade.

Chet and Joe stopped to listen. In the distance, voices were shouting in unison, "Here comes the King! Here comes the King!"

144

Leaving the fireworks, the boys hurried back in the direction of the parade.

"Maybe Duboise is riding on a float as the voodoo king," Joe speculated.

"I don't see how that's possible," Frank replied. "He's at his club. Unless he left early."

"It isn't the voodoo king at all!" Joe cried as the boys finally broke through the crowd far enough to see the parade. "It's King George!"

"You're right!" the older Hardy exclaimed, peering over the other spectators' heads.

Down the avenue, on the summit of a regally decorated float, sat a man on a big throne. He had on a white powdered wig, red coat, and wore a thin mask over his eyes. From his perch, he waved grandly at the onlookers, many of whom joined in the chorus of voices shouting, "Here comes the King!"

"How do you know it's supposed to be King George?" Chet asked.

"Because it says so right on the float," Frank replied.

The plump boy stood on his toes, trying to see far enough over the crowd. Finally, he was able to make out the sparkling gold letters, which read KING GEORGE III OF ENGLAND.

"So Clem didn't lie," Frank said thoughtfully.

"King George really rides in one of the Mardi Gras parades."

Joe chuckled. "If you go by the sheriff's theory, it's Clem himself sitting up there. With that wig and mask it could be anyone, including Dad!"

"Well, I think we can eliminate that possibility," Frank said. "But I *would* like to know who it is."

"Me, too," his brother agreed. "Maybe some of these people will fill us in."

A couple of onlookers near the boys were chanting "Here comes the King!" as the float cruised by. One of them was dressed in a gaudy Uncle Sam outfit and was shouting as if he knew the ritual well.

Frank asked him about the man on the float.

"Oh, yes," he replied above the noise. "King George rises out of the swamp every year just to come to Mardi Gras. I've been here for the last five years, and the King makes it every time."

"Seems like he's become a celebrity around here," Frank went on, fishing for more information.

But the man in the Uncle Sam getup had lost interest in continuing the conversation. He began snapping his fingers and moving his feet to the music in the air.

"Let's ask someone else," Joe suggested to his brother.

They walked through the crowd, questioning other people on King George. After a while, they

147

realized that nobody seemed to know who was playing the King in the parade.

"Well, there's one more thing we can do to find out," Frank said. "Remember Clem told us he followed the King to a party? At first, I paid no attention to it, figuring all this was a figment of Clem's imagination. But now I'm beginning to think he really saw this King, and perhaps there's a party, too!"

"If we can get to the end of the parade before the float, we should be able to shadow this guy," Joe said excitedly. "Come on!"

"You two go ahead," Chet said. He had started to lag behind with a case of tired legs. "I'm going back to the club to sit down."

Without Chet, the Hardys made better time through the crowd. They figured that the end of the parade was no more than another mile down the avenue, and if they got there in time, they would be able to catch King George as he climbed off his float.

But when they arrived at the spot, the float had already arrived and was empty.

"Oh, nuts!" Joe growled. "We missed him!"

Frank turned red with anger. "Well, there ought to be an official around here somewhere who can tell us who the King is."

Several men were at work at the parade's end

point, directing the floats and marching bands as they were brought to a halt. The boys walked over to the man who seemed to be in charge.

"We don't know who this particular King is," he said, bringing a big cigar butt to his lips. "Maybe you could check with the organization that sponsored this parade."

"Which one is that?" Joe asked.

"Somebody in the Park Services Department would be able to tell you. They help private groups put the activities together."

Disappointed, Frank and Joe returned to the jazz club. They looked for Stretch, hoping to go over his song again to figure out whether the changed wording was indeed part of a secret message between Duboise and Stokes. But the trombonist wasn't there.

Frank used the wall phone to call Bayport. His father was out, and his mother advised him to call Sam Radley, Mr. Hardy's operative who was now helping him on the burglary case. "He may have some news for you," she concluded.

"Thanks, Mom," Frank said, then dialed Radley's number.

"I found out something for you." Sam's cheerful voice sounded over the wire. "One of Mann's frequent passengers is Durby McPhee, the last art dealer who had his gallery robbed."

"Durby McPhee?" Frank asked. "Are you serious?"

"I certainly am," Radley told him. "It may be just a coincidence. But it seems like a pretty big one."

"Thanks, Sam," Frank said and hung up. Then he told Joe what Radley had said.

"Durby McPhee?" Joe said in disbelief. "He's one of the victims. How could he possibly be involved with the burglars?"

"Well, perhaps Mann is the crook, and his passengers are not involved. He probably knew McPhee owned a gallery, so he robbed him."

Joe shook his head. "I don't know. It all sounds crazy."

The two boys returned to their room, expecting to find Chet in bed. But he wasn't there.

"I wonder where he went," Joe said, worried. "Stretch isn't around either."

Just then, Frank's eye caught sight of a piece of paper on the bed. It was a note, which he read aloud to his brother:

IF YOU WANT TO SEE A REALLY BIG
BOOMER, GO BACK TO THE PARADE. CHET.

"A big boomer?" Joe asked, scrunching up his face with curiosity.

"Come on!" Frank said. "Whatever it is, I don't want to miss it!"

16 A Strange Picnic

Bounding down the stairs, Frank and Joe were out of the club and back to the parade in a couple of minutes.

"How're we going to find Chet in this crowd?" Joe asked, scanning the thousands of people who filled the avenue.

His brother chuckled. "Let's just watch the parade. I have a hunch Chet and Stretch are in this together."

The two looked at the passing floats, their heads swimming with anticipation. They didn't have to wait long before the sound of dixieland jazz could be heard down the street.

"There they are!" Joe yelled in a burst of excitement. "The big boomer is Chet!"

Marching down the street and pounding on a big bass drum, Chet led the way for Stretch's band. Frank and Joe nearly fell over with laughter at the sight of their chubby friend having his biggest night of the year, and they cheered wildly as the jazzmen started to pass by.

Stretch's band was playing a fast version of "Swing Low, Sweet Chariot," with Stretch sliding out the jazzed-up melody on his trombone. Other musicians took their turns playing solo improvisations, until, in the last verse, they all played together again. Chet, meanwhile, was hamming it up on the bass drum.

Frank and Joe followed the marching band, which went a few blocks down the street, then broke away from the parade and returned to Stretch's.

"Hey, big boomer," Joe quipped when Chet finally joined them. "Where'd you find the drum?"

"It's Stretch's," the boy answered. "He used to play it in his high-school band."

"Don't you think he has a great music career ahead of him?" Stretch beamed as he joined the boys. "He looked pretty good out there in the parade."

The Hardys slapped their buddy on the back, then led him inside and up the stairs. In their room, they were asleep almost as soon as they hit their pillows.

In the morning, the boys made their way through the crowded streets to the Park Services office. To their chagrin, however, they found out that all government agencies were closed on Fat Tuesday.

Frank banged his forehead with the palm of his hand. "I should have thought of that," he said. "I knew it, but I forgot all about it."

"Well, that settles that," Chet said. "Why don't we go out and watch the festivities for a while?"

The boys did that until Frank said, "Hey, we've wasted enough time. Let's visit Sedgwick Stokes. Perhaps that'll give us another clue."

Chet looked at his watch. "He's probably out to lunch, like we should be," he said.

"Maybe so. Let's try anyway."

When the boys arrived at the real-estate office, the door was locked.

"See, I told you so," Chet said.

Frank nodded absently and surveyed the hallway floor. "I thought I saw something on the way—ah, there it is!" He walked back a few steps and picked up a crumpled-up ball of paper.

"What is it?" Joe said and glanced over Frank's shoulder.

"Looks like a map."

"Maybe that little cross there is where Stokes is right now," Joe suggested.

Frank nodded. "It seems to me that these are directions to some place outside town," he declared, and folded the piece of paper, then stuffed it in his shirt pocket. "Stretch may know where it is," he added.

The trio left the office and walked back to the club. The trombonist was in his little office filling out a ledger sheet.

"See what you can make of this," Frank said, laying the piece of paper on the desk.

Stretch studied the map for a moment, then looked up. "Sure, it's the same road we took to the Gumbo Diner. But this leads three or four miles past it and up another road."

"May we borrow your car for the afternoon?" Joe asked. "We'd like to check the place out."

"Be my guest," Stretch told him, handing over the keys. "Just try to stay out of trouble."

A half-hour later, the young detectives drove past the Gumbo Diner and into densely forested countryside. Then Joe turned left on a gravel lane, following it until he came upon a number of cars parked next to a field.

"Wow!" Chet exclaimed. "We've come to the right place!"

A huge cookout was in progress in the field, with over a hundred people clustered around tables that

154

smoked and steamed with the odor of good food. The boys climbed out of the car and warily joined the crowd.

"It's heaven!" Chet cried happily, looking around him. Large pots of shrimp bubbled over the open fires. Barbecued chicken and spareribs covered long grills over burning coals, and pots were filled with fish and vegetables, rice and hot peppers.

"Hold on to your tummy," Frank teased Chet. "We weren't invited, so don't help yourself."

Just then, a man at one of the barbecue pits waved the boys over. "You look mighty hungry," he said in a thick creole accent. "You better get plates quick and eat something before it's all gone."

"We've just been invited," Chet said, grinning from ear to ear.

Without losing a second, he picked up a plate. Then he went from table to table, heaping it high with food. Frank and Joe also took something, but more because they wanted to appear as guests than out of hunger.

The guests at the cookout were a mixed group. Many spoke with a creole accent, a singsong Haitian language that had its roots in the French language.

"I wonder if Stokes is around here somewhere," Joe said, threading through the people.

"There he is," Frank told him.

The small-framed, real-estate investor was seated at one of the picnic tables with a group of other men.

"Hey, one of these guys is the one who slugged me at Stretch's the first night we were in town!" Joe exclaimed.

"So this is the voodoo crowd," Chet said. "Maybe we should hurry up and eat and then get out of here!"

"Oh, no," Frank said with a chuckle. "We came here to see if we could pick up a clue, didn't we? Let's stay a while and watch these birds."

"Look, the guy whose mask I pulled off at the club when I got hit is getting up from the table," Joe said. "He's heading toward the woods, it seems!"

"Chet, you stay here and keep an eye on Stokes," Frank said. "We're going to follow this man, okay?"

Chet was not happy with his assignment, but then he decided that this way he could finish his lunch.

"Sure, go ahead," he agreed.

Staying a safe distance from the man, who was big enough to take both boys on in a fight, Frank and Joe found themselves on a narrow path cut through the shrubbery. It led to an old shack with boarded-up windows.

The hut was the size of a large garage, and when the man opened the door to go inside, the Hardys could hear a chorus of voices shouting from within.

"What's going on in there?" Joe wondered aloud as they drew near the shack.

"I don't know," Frank replied, puzzled by the loud voices. "Maybe we can take a peek through the door and find out."

The two detectives cautiously made their way to the side of the building. Then they crept along the wall, rounding the corner to the front.

"Here goes," Frank whispered as he grasped the door and pulled it open a few inches.

17 With a Little Bit of Luck

Frank quickly peered through the door, then shut it again. "A lot of people are in there," he whispered to Joe. "They're watching something going on in the center of the room."

"Do you think we could sneak in without being noticed?" Joe asked.

"Probably. It's dark enough, and everyone's too caught up with whatever's going on to notice anything else."

The Hardys waited until the shouts were at a high point, then quickly slipped through the door and ducked into a corner of the room. In a few moments, their eyes had adjusted to the darkness. In the middle of the shack was a small, fenced-in arena, where two roosters were engaged in combat.

One of them wore a bright red vest, the other a small tricornered hat!

"It's a cockfight!" Frank whispered excitedly to his brother, referring to the outdated sport of pitting two roosters against each other in a deadly battle.

"It's gruesome," Joe added, wrinkling up his nose at the sight. "But why the costumes?"

"I guess one is supposed to be a British soldier, the other an American Revolutionary," the older boy replied.

"Just like Rattlesnake Clem and King George," Joe put in, excitement growing in his voice. "Maybe there's a connection."

"Maybe you're—" Frank started to say, then stopped in midsentence. He pointed to the wall. "Look at that stuff over there!"

Joe focused his eyes on a shelf near the back of the room. It was filled with silver cups.

"Trophies!" Joe whispered. "Those must be prizes for the cockfight winners."

"They don't look like regular trophies to me," Frank stated. "I think they're differently shaped silver cups, probably stolen. I'm going to have a look."

Crawling on his hands and knees, he worked his way to the far side of the shack, where he began to inspect the prizes.

Just then, a final cheer broke from the crowd as the fight ended. One of the cocks strutted triumphantly around the ring. The other lay dead and bloody from the bout. Money began to exchange hands as the winners collected their bets.

A man broke away from the crowd and started toward the shelf. "Hey! There's one of those nosy kids who're staying with Stretch!" he yelled. "Quick! Get him!"

Before Frank had a chance to retreat, three men grabbed him and tied him up.

"And there's another one!" came a shout from the group around the ring when Joe made a dash for the door. The blond sleuth was halfway there when several of the men were on top of him. Joe tried to break free, but was soon overpowered.

Duboise stepped out of the shadows and faced the young detectives. "You just don't know when to call it quits!" He smiled evilly. "Well, as they say, curiosity killed the cat." His grin seemed to grow even wider as a thought occurred to him. "Put them in the ring," he ordered.

Laughter broke out among the men. "In the ring!" several of them shouted, catching on to what their leader had in mind.

Frank and Joe were shoved into the cockfighting arena.

"I'll bet on the blond kid!" one of the men called out.

"I'll take the other one!" another man shouted.

Frank glared at Duboise. "Do you think we're going to fight each other?"

"Yes," Duboise said, his smile not leaving his face. "Because you have no choice. You see, if you boys don't fight each other, neither one of you is going to leave here alive. You will fight until one of you knocks the other out. And I'll know it if you try and fake it."

The sleuths gasped in disbelief. They had fought their way out of many tough situations before, but had never been pitted against each other!

Once all the bets had been placed, Duboise rang the bell to mark the beginning of the fight.

Immediately, Frank leaped on top of his brother and brought him to the ground! A chorus of cheers followed as the youths wrestled in the dirt.

"Hey, not so rough," Joe whispered in Frank's ear when they were locked together in such a way that the men couldn't hear them.

"Sorry. I had to make it look good," the older sleuth whispered back. "These guys have no intention of letting us go, even if we do fight."

"I know."

"When I say the word 'police,' we'll both run for the door. It's our only chance."

161

"Okay."

Frank and Joe broke from their wrestling hold and got to their feet. Joe took a swing at Frank, which the older boy blocked with his arm. Then Frank faked a blow to his brother's stomach and Joe pretended to double up in pain.

Suddenly, Frank stopped fighting and pointed at one of the men in the crowd. "I know you!" he yelled. "You're an undercover agent!" The gang surrounding the ring turned menacingly on the man.

The man threw up his hands in confusion. "Undercover agent? I don't know what you're . . ."

"Yes, you are! I saw you at headquarters talking to Chief Lloyd the other day. You're with the police!"

With the men nearing a frenzied state, Frank and Joe leaped from the ring and bolted for the door. One of the crooks managed to grab Joe's arm at the door, but the sleuth answered with an upper cut to the man's jaw. And this time he wasn't faking it!

Before the others could lay a hand on them, the two boys were running from the shack and back down the path toward the picnic site. Chet was working on his third helping of food when his buddies found him.

"Where have you been?" the plump boy asked,

surprised to see Frank and Joe panting with exhaustion.

"Never mind," Frank told him. "We have to get out of here, pronto."

Realizing it was urgent, Chet dropped his plate and the trio raced to Stretch's car. Frank slid behind the wheel and they took off before their pursuers reached them.

"Wow!" Chet cried, staring at the angry men through the rear window. "What was that all about?"

Quickly, Frank and Joe filled him in on what happened, then Joe asked his brother, "Did you get any clue at the shelf?"

"They weren't trophies," Frank told him. "At least not the usual kind handed out at athletic events. They were all sterling silver hollowware, and some of them had names and dates inscribed. Should be easy to check if they were stolen."

"Let's stop off at the police," Joe suggested. "Maybe the list we gave the chief will contain one or more of the items."

"I think it will," Frank said. Then he reached into his pocket and produced some clothlike material. "Guess what this is."

Joe took the small piece of cloth and puzzled over it. "What is it?"

Frank grinned. "I'll give you a hint. It's the answer to a mystery we couldn't solve before we left home."

Now Joe was more puzzled than ever. He stared at the cloth, inspecting the way it was knit and how the seams were cut. "This is a piece of a sock," he said. "What does that—" Suddenly, his eyes lit up. "This belongs to Dad!"

The boys recognized the sock not only by its peculiar design, but also by a tiny yellow paint spot that had dried into the material.

"It's Dad's sock all right," Frank agreed. "He was painting the porch a couple of weeks ago."

"But what was it doing in a cockfight shack on the outskirts of New Orleans?" Joe wondered.

Frank became serious. "There was a collection of voodoo dolls on the shelves beside the other stuff. When I saw one wearing an outfit that looked like a sock, I took it off and stuffed it in my pocket."

Joe shook his head, hardly believing that his father's sock had actually been stolen for a voodoo doll. "Somebody wanted to put a hex on Dad!"

"Right," Frank agreed grimly. "What beats me is how one of those guys sneaked in our house and took it."

"Durby McPhee!" Joe exclaimed. "He was in Dad's study on the evening before the sock was missing."

"He excused himself when we were talking to Dad about the stakeout, remember?" Frank added excitedly.

The Hardys were more confused than ever. Why one of the burglary victims would steal a sock for a voodoo doll was hard to imagine. Yet, this was the second time McPhee had become the subject of suspicion.

"I'm beginning to think that these mysteries might be connected," Frank went on. "It's more than coincidence that both the voodoo case and the burglary case led to New Orleans."

"With the clues you've been finding lately, I bet you're right," Chet put in.

As the boys continued driving, they slowly began to realize they had lost their way. In their rush to get away from the picnic, Frank had made a wrong turn down the highway. After winding in circles for a while, they noticed a sign indicating the way back to the city by a different route.

"This is a real old road," Chet said, looking out the window as they passed tree-shaded mansions that apparently hadn't been lived in for many years.

"Few people can afford to keep up these places nowadays," Frank commented. "Maybe I'll get rich some day and move here to retire."

Joe chuckled and gazed idly around the scenery.

"There's one house still in use," he said, pointing to a huge property as they drove by.

It was alive with activity. Workers were outside cutting the bushes and lawns. Curtains were being hung in the windows. Two men carried a big glass chandelier through the front door, and boxes stood all over the place.

"Someone's planning to live in style," Chet said, impressed by the display of wealth.

"Stop the car!" Joe cried suddenly.

"Why?" Frank asked, alarmed by Joe's outburst.

"Just stop!"

Frank put on the brakes and pulled to the side of the road a short way past the mansion. Then, at his brother's urging, he backed up until they were next to the driveway.

Joe pointed to a small brass plaque imbedded in the stone front gate. "That's what I thought I saw!"

"Belle Lee!" Chet cried, reading the words out loud. "This mansion must be the Belle Lee Duboise was talking about in that song!"

Frank turned the car and headed up the driveway, also wondering whether it might be the place Duboise referred to in the lyrics he had added to Stretch's song. "If those words really were a message," he said, "we may be on to something here."

Pulling up next to the front door, the boys hopped from the car.

"Is somebody moving in here?" Frank asked one of the workers who was carrying a box inside.

The man stopped. "I don't know. All I know is that somebody is throwing a Fat Tuesday party tonight. A masked ball!"

18 The Masked Ball

Just then, another man appeared in the doorway. He was thin, but his face was rounded and flat, giving his whole body the look of a ball sitting on top of a long stick.

"This is private property," he told the visitors gruffly.

"Sorry," Frank apologized. "We were just sight-seeing in the area, and when we saw what was going on here, we decided to drop in. It's such a neat place, we thought maybe we could have a look around."

"You may not have a look around!" the man said, glaring at the sleuths.

"One of the workers told us you were having a

party here," Joe said, trying to keep up the conversation as long as possible.

The man looked sharply at the boys. "Do I have to throw you kids out? I told you to leave and I meant it."

Just then, one of the hired help stuck his head out the front door. "Where do you want me to put the punch bowl, Mr. Mann?" he asked.

"The corner of the ballroom," came the quick answer.

Suddenly, it dawned on Frank and Joe that they had been speaking with Roger Mann, the Cessna's pilot! Joe was about to open his mouth, but Frank gave him a quick glance that told him not to, and the boys left without another word.

"That guy was Roger Mann!" Joe said excitedly, when they were back in the car and on their way down the driveway. "We finally found him, and you want to go away without any questions?"

"Right," his brother told him. "I think we've stumbled on the key to this mystery, and I don't want to blow it!"

"So what'll we do?" Chet asked.

"We find ourselves some costumes and crash the party tonight."

Joe snapped his fingers as he realized that Frank was thinking. "King George is having his masked ball at Belle Lee!"

"Right." Frank grinned.

"So Rattlesnake Clem was right after all!" Chet concluded. "There really is a King George, and he's having another party!"

"That's what it looks like," Frank said, steering Stretch's car back down the road. "And he's probably Roger Mann's passenger."

"Which means he couldn't be Clem," Chet said. "He was in jail when that plane left Swamp Creek."

"It also means that Duboise and his voodoo gang are mixed up with this King George character," Frank added.

Once they were back in downtown New Orleans, the boys went to the police and told them what they had found in the cockfight shack.

"And you think those objects were stolen from art galleries?" Chief Lloyd asked.

"I saw some silver hollowware that may correspond to the description of the list I gave you," Frank said.

"Okay, give me the directions to the place, will you?"

Frank did, but asked the chief not to move in on the gang just yet. After some argument, the officer finally relented.

"All right, since you're the sons of Fenton Hardy, I'll go along with you and wait till the morning. But if you find the burglars, I want you to call me immediately."

The boys promised to do so, then they left the station. They returned to Stretch's club and told the trombonist what they had learned. Then they started to make costumes that would conceal them at the masked ball in the evening.

"How do I look?" Chet asked, having dressed up like an Arab sheik.

"Stunning and well-fed," Frank teased. "How about us?"

Both boys wore powdered wigs and ruffled shirts that Stretch had dug up for them from his Mardi Gras costume drawer. They also had on black masks much like the one King George had worn in the parade.

"Dashing!" Chet laughed at the disguises.

The boys had dinner and made plans for getting into the mansion without being noticed. After discussing various alternatives, Frank finally got up. "It's time," he said, looking at his watch. "Let's go!"

They put the finishing touches on their outfits, then again got in Stretch's car and headed for Belle Lee. Frank parked on the side of the road some distance away, the boys slipped on their masks, and the costumed trio looped around through the woods until they were behind the house.

The mansion was full of people in elaborate costumes; many also strolled around the grounds.

171

The boys spotted some guests entering and leaving through the back door.

"Let's sneak in that way," Joe suggested.

"Not so fast," his brother warned. "There's a guy guarding the entrance."

Taking a closer look, Joe noticed that one of the costumed people was standing by the door, watching the others as they came and went.

"We need a decoy, just as I thought," Frank decided and turned to Chet. "Here's your chance to show us what you can do."

During their earlier discussion, Chet had volunteered to be the decoy, if necessary, and draw attention from Frank and Joe while they sneaked into the masked ball. But he had hoped it would not be necessary.

"What do I do?" he asked reluctantly.

"Simple," Joe said. "Just go close to the door, and when the guard spots you, run. We'll meet you back at the car later."

Halfheartedly, Chet strolled around the lawn, slowly making his way to the door. Frank and Joe went in the other direction, then cut back toward the door on the opposite side.

The guard finally saw Chet, and watched suspiciously as the boy in the sheik costume came closer.

"Hey you!" the guard shouted at last. "Let me see your invitation!"

Chet didn't delay another second! Picking his robe up over his knees, he ran toward the woods. The guard hesitated for a moment, not sure whether to leave his post. Then, making a decision, he bolted from the doorway after the intruder.

Frank and Joe walked casually inside the mansion.

"I hope that guy doesn't catch him," Joe murmured.

"Don't worry," Frank said. "He won't want to leave his post for long, and Chet is fast when he wants to be."

Once they were inside, the Hardys mingled with the other revelers. The ballroom was decorated like an old southern mansion, with paintings of English royalty hung along the walls. A string quartet played waltz music while a number of the guests danced. Many were dressed as eighteenth-century English noblemen. The rest were in a variety of Mardi Gras costumes. All were masked.

King George himself sat on a throne at one end of the ballroom. After a few minutes, he stood up from his throne and left the room. The boys tried to follow him, but by the time they were out in the hallway, he was gone.

"Where did he go?" Joe said in frustration.

Frank scanned the hallway for signs of the King, until his eyes landed on a stairway leading to the second floor. "Remember the other words Duboise added to Stretch's song?" he said excitedly.

"Yes," Joe replied. "It went, 'Gold and silver will be waiting there, in a sunlit room up a winding stair.'" He pointed. "But that's not a winding stair. It goes straight up to the second floor."

"I know," the older boy said quickly. "But I bet there's a winding stairway somewhere in this place."

Going in opposite directions, the two searched the first floor. Having no luck, they met again in the hall.

"Nothing here," Joe said.

"No. Let's go upstairs."

The second floor was quiet and the rooms were empty of people or furniture. Frank and Joe again scouted around for the "winding stair" mentioned in Duboise's song.

"I found it!" Frank suddenly called from around a bend in the hall.

Joe, who had been searching the rooms at the other end, joined his brother at the foot of a narrow spiral staircase. "You found it all right," he said with hushed excitement.

Careful not to make a sound, the boys crept up the stairs. Voices were audible from behind a small door at the top, and the young detectives stopped to listen.

"Everything on this table is yours, Stokes," a man said. "Duboise, that table is yours. You may split it up with your men any way you want it."

"And what do I get?" another man pleaded.

"I'll pay you when we get back to Bayport, Roger," came the reply.

"Sounds like the King is splitting up his booty," Frank whispered.

"Now's the perfect time to nab those guys," Joe whispered back.

"No," his brother cautioned. "There are at least four of them and only two of us. We wouldn't stand a chance."

"So we'll call the police," Joe said.

"And we'll have to move fast. The police—" Frank's sentence was cut off as the small attic door opened with a jerk!

19 Attic Brawl

Before the Hardys had time to react, a strong hand grabbed Joe by the collar and yanked him into the room!

"It's those kids again!" Duboise spat, throwing Joe to the floor.

Frank leaped into the room, making a flying tackle on the voodoo leader. But in another second, all the men were on top of the sleuths, pinning them to the floor.

The attic room was crammed with stolen property. Boxes of silverware, expensive lamps and vases, valuable paintings, and an assortment of knick-knacks cluttered the floor and tables.

"The police will be here any minute!" Joe threatened the thieves.

"And if they are, they won't find anything, including you two!" the King hissed.

The boy stared up at the masked man who stood over him threateningly. In spite of the mask, the King seemed familiar to Joe, and the young detective strained to think of where he had seen him before.

Frank was pinned down by Roger Mann and Sedgwick Stokes, who gripped the boy roughly, waiting for instructions on what to do with him.

Just then, the attic window flew open and several diamondback rattlesnakes were hurled into the room!

"It's Clem!" Frank shouted as the old man swung through the opening. He wore a buckskin jacket and his tricornered hat, and to make his entrance more dramatic, he let out a bloodcurdling scream!

Jumping up to avoid the rattlers, the men let go of the two captives. Frank and Joe immediately got to their feet and prepared to fight.

"So we meet again," the King growled at Clem. "Only this time you won't get away, Clemson."

"I'm the Swamp Fox!" the old man bellowed. "And I've come to take back the taxes which rightfully belong to the colonies!"

"This is the second time you've crashed my party. I will put an end to this!"

"We'll see about that!" Clem yelled, advancing on King George, rattlesnake in hand.

Neither of the men intended to give up without a fight. Moments later, the attic room became a flurry of fists, with everyone both fighting and trying to avoid the snakes on the floor.

Joe knocked Stokes out cold with one well-placed jab to the jaw, but he found Duboise to be a much tougher match. In the meantime, Frank had taken on Roger Mann, who turned out to be a strong fighter.

Chet appeared suddenly at the door, still dressed in his sheik outfit. Seeing that Joe was having a hard time with Duboise, he jumped into the fray and started swinging.

With the scales now tipped against them, the men tried to break free and scramble for the door. But as they did, the police chief and his men met them on the stairway!

"These are the burglars!" Frank called down to the officers. "The evidence is all here."

It didn't take long before the chief had the men in his custody. He made them march up the stairs and back into the room, where he looked over the collection of stolen property. "We'll have to check this stuff out down at the precinct," he said, "but I'm sure we've got the right crooks. Good thing

Chet notified us. He got worried after you didn't show up for a while."

"I didn't steal any of this stuff," Stokes protested, now recovered from Joe's blow to his chin. "Roger Mann and the King brought it all down here."

"There's a law against dealing in stolen property," Chief Lloyd told him, "whether you stole it yourself or not."

Frank took a step toward the King. "I've been wanting to do this for days," he said, pulling the mask from the man's face.

"Durby McPhee!" he gasped, recognizing the gaunt, red-headed gallery owner. "I don't believe it!"

McPhee glared at him. "Then don't!"

"Why did you burglarize your own shop?" Joe queried. "And what is this King George charade all about?"

McPhee was furious. "You figure it out," he said and ended with a string of curses.

"I—I know everything," Stokes sputtered. "Will you go easy on me if I tell you?"

"I can't promise you anything," the chief said. "But I must advise you to speak the truth." He read the real-estate broker his rights. Close to panic, Stokes hesitated, then pointed an accusing finger at McPhee.

"He—he's the big-shot thief. He robbed various

galleries—the ones he knew had good stuff that he wanted."

"Shut up!" McPhee thundered, but Stokes was not to be stopped. He was shaking with fright and all he was interested in was getting out of trouble as best he could.

"But why did he burglarize his own shop?" Joe asked.

"He told me he became worried when he heard your father got involved in the case. Then he had the brilliant idea to frame Clem. You see, Clem had followed him last year after the parade. The old geezer had the crazy notion that McPhee was really King George who levied excessive taxes on the people. Anyway, Clem crashed our party and caused a lot of trouble. Durby tried to do him in, but he got away. It took Durby a long time to find out where he lived. McPhee was afraid that Clem could pose a real danger to the operation because he knew too much."

"Did Clem know who the King really was?"

"I doubt it. After he crashed the party, we chased him off the property, then kept a close watch. He didn't come back. But Durby wanted to be absolutely sure Clem wouldn't talk."

"So he tried to get rid of Clem?" Joe asked.

Stokes nodded. "When he found out your father got involved in the case, he had the brilliant idea to frame Clem. That would have eliminated the old troublemaker and gotten your father off his back at the same time."

"Shut up, I tell you!" McPhee shouted, but Stokes only shrugged.

"I get it," Frank said. "McPhee flew down to Georgia, and brought back some of Clem's rattlers. He asked us to stake out his gallery, then arrived himself, wearing a tricornered hat and carrying the rattlers in a bag."

"Right!" Joe put in. "And when we followed him into the parking lot and couldn't find him, he was really inside the place! Of course, he had a key to let himself in. Then he opened the window."

Frank nodded. "So we run off in different directions, while McPhee walks out the front door, leaves it open for the cop to see, drops the rattlers in our car, and goes home! Boy, were we duped!"

"He knew we were going to the carnival," Joe took up the story, "because we told him when he came to our house. So he planted the snake oil in the sack he conveniently left for us to find near the gallery. This, he figured, would confuse us . . . maybe make us suspect someone at the carnival. So all he had to do was to pay the snake charmer a small fee to point us to Clem."

"Brilliant," Chet said glumly.

Frank nodded. "When we were hot on Clem's

trail and flew to Savannah, he had Roger Mann take
him into Swamp Creek and planted the King's
costume and the stuff he had taken from his shop in
Clem's garage. No doubt he wrote the fake note to
Rick because he figured the longer we stayed in the
swamp, the better!"

Chet chuckled. "And to confuse everyone even
more, he walked around the swamp in that crazy
King George getup and made sure people saw
him."

"That certainly reinforced Clem's idea about the
King," Joe said. "And when Clem got arrested,
McPhee wanted to make sure he sounded crazy
enough, so no one would believe him if he said
anything about the party in New Orleans."

"Which brings us back to this," Frank said,
gesturing at the merchandise in the room. "What's
this all about, Mr. Stokes?"

"Duboise and I leased the place for a month and
arranged the party. Everyone knew it was to be
held in this area the night of Fat Tuesday, but no
one knew which mansion. Maurice played a song at
the club a particular night during Mardi Gras, so
those people who were supposed to attend would
know where to go."

"You mean, last year the masked ball was somewhere else?"

"That's right. We couldn't get the place back

183

on a short-term lease, so we took this one."

"But why the party?" Frank inquired.

"That had a double purpose," Stokes went on. "Earlier in the afternoon, McPhee and his distributors went through all the stuff that had been stolen and planned who was to get rid of what and where. Then he treated them and their friends to a party, where he paid me and Duboise off for arranging everything."

McPhee's head had sunk between his shoulders during Stokes's testimony. He knew he was caught and had become very quiet.

Frank noticed his change in expression and turned to him. "Tell us, Mr. McPhee, how did you ever think up this King George charade?"

McPhee shrugged helplessly. "I've been attending Mardi Gras for many years now," he said, "and somewhere along the line started to play King George. It was a hobby of mine. I became a local celebrity of sorts. They put me in the parade and made me a star."

"And to hold your annual meeting at the end of Mardi Gras in a city crowded with strangers, where nobody would be looking for you, fitted in perfectly," Joe added.

"Of course. No one took any notice when I shipped my loot down here. It was a safe place."

"You're a businessman," Joe said. "You've had that shop in Bayport for a number of years. Didn't you make enough money without resorting to theft?"

McPhee shrugged. "I did for the longest time. Then I made a few bad investments. In order to avoid going out of business, I figured I'd pull a few burglaries to get me back on my feet again. That was a couple of years ago. Then the theft business worked out so well—"

"Real well," Chet couldn't help but put in.

McPhee shrugged. "You win, you lose."

"If you're finished questioning, I'll take them down to the station," Chief Lloyd said when everyone had fallen quiet.

"I have one more thing I'd like to ask," Joe said. "How did our father's sock end up on a voodoo doll?" He pulled out the remains of the sock and showed it to McPhee.

The man chuckled. "That was Duboise's idea. When your father got on the case, I told the people here that I was worried. I even considered canceling the party this year. Turns out I should have!"

"Ah, but Stokes and Duboise didn't want that," Joe said. "They would have lost their commission. So instead, Duboise promised you to take care of my father by putting a hex on him?"

185

"He did. And I thought it certainly couldn't hurt," McPhee admitted.

"When you came to our house, you excused yourself while in Dad's study and got the sock from the laundry basket in the bathroom?"

"Sure. It was easy."

"How'd you ever meet Stokes and Duboise?" Frank asked.

"During Mardi Gras many years ago," McPhee replied. "I made those guys rich by having them work for me!"

"That's how they got their money to invest in all those clubs," Frank deduced.

"After Duboise decided to harass the club owners into selling at a cheap price with his voodoo gang. He wanted Jazz Alley to be the only show in town, didn't he?" Chet challenged.

Duboise gave him a cold look. "It wasn't just my idea. Stokes and I are partners, remember?"

"Oh, we won't forget, don't worry," the chief said. While he and his men led the criminals downstairs, Frank turned to Joe. "Jazz Alley will probably be closed now, and a lot of its business will go to Stretch."

"I sure hope so," his brother said with a grin. "Stretch deserves it." When the three boys got back to the club that night, they found their friend cleaning his trombone onstage.

"We've got good news for you," Joe called out, and they told him what had happened.

The old jazz musician grinned from ear to ear. "Boys, I can't thank you enough for what you've done," he said.

"Don't mention it," Frank said. "We had a wonderful time in New Orleans. Now let me call the airport and see when we can get a flight home." He went to the telephone and returned a few minutes later. "We're leaving at nine in the morning. And thanks again for putting us up, Stretch."

The old man nodded, his eyes suddenly sad. "I hate to see you go," he said softly. "But when you get back to Bayport, tell my grandson that everything is all right down here now."

"We will," Frank promised, shaking Stretch's hand.

Early next morning, the boys left the deserted club with their bags in their hands. They had decided not to call Mr. Hardy ahead of time, but to surprise him instead.

"Hey, we forgot to thank Clem," Chet said suddenly. "After all, he saved your necks last night."

"He's probably back on his way to Swamp Creek. I saw him sneak away while the police were questioning Stokes and McPhee," Frank said. "The case against him will be dropped, and I bet he's happy to have won his battle with the King."

"Hey, boys!" A voice sounded behind him. They turned to see Stretch running after them down the street. "I came to the club to give you a ride to the airport. Almost missed ya!"

The young detectives turned and followed the old man to his car. In a short while, they were boarding an airliner. Stretch stayed to watch the takeoff, waving to the plane as it lifted off the ground.

By evening, Frank and Joe were back home. Their father was, indeed, surprised to see them and listened with pride as they told him about the mystery. Then they phoned Peter Walker to say that his grandfather's troubles were over.

"How can I ever repay you?" the relieved basketball star asked.

Joe chuckled. "Just help us win more games. We needed to get your mind off voodoo and back on the team for next season!"

When he hung up, Joe wondered if they would ever solve a mystery again. Even though he didn't know it yet, there would be one right in their own town of Bayport called *The Billion Dollar Ransom*.

He looked up and saw Aunt Gertrude standing in the door. "Guess what, Aunty," he called out. "We found Dad's missing sock!"

"You did?" she asked, puzzled. "You weren't even here!"

"Neither was the sock," Joe said. "It was on a voodoo doll."

Gertrude Hardy's mouth dropped open at the sight of the tattered material. "What!"

"It was supposed to put a hex on Dad," Joe explained. "But don't worry about it. It didn't work."

Miss Hardy shook her head. "The things that happen in this business are just unbelievable."

THE HARDY BOYS® SERIES
by Franklin W. Dixon

Night of the Werewolf (#59)
Mystery of the Samurai Sword (#60)
The Pentagon Spy (#61)
The Apeman's Secret (#62)
The Mummy Case (#63)
Mystery of Smugglers Cove (#64)
The Stone Idol (#65)
The Vanishing Thieves (#66)
The Outlaw's Silver (#67)
The Submarine Caper (#68)
The Four-Headed Dragon (#69)
The Infinity Clue (#70)
Track of the Zombie (#71)
The Voodoo Plot (#72)
The Billion Dollar Ransom (#73)
Tic-Tac-Terror (#74)

You will also enjoy

THE TOM SWIFT® SERIES
by Victor Appleton

The City in the Stars (#1)
Terror on the Moons of Jupiter (#2)
The Alien Probe (#3)
The War in Outer Space (#4)
The Astral Fortress (#5)
The Rescue Mission (#6)
Ark Two (#7)

You are invited to join

THE OFFICIAL NANCY DREW ®/
HARDY BOYS ® FAN CLUB!

Be the first in your neighborhood to find out
about the newest adventures of Nancy, Frank,
and Joe in the **Nancy Drew** ®/ **Hardy Boys** ®
Mystery Reporter, and to receive your official
membership card. Just send your name, age,
address, and zip code on a postcard *only* to:

The Official Nancy Drew ®/
Hardy Boys ® **Fan Club**
Wanderer Books
Simon & Schuster Building
1230 Avenue of the Americas
New York, New York 10020